What the critics are saying...

"A compelling read...passionate narrative, heavily erotic. Demonstrates some of the most gripping elements of the power exchange that is the basis of relationships that have the dynamic of Domination and submission." ~ *Sensual Romance.*

"Gold star a phenomenal job at depicting the seduction of the world of BDSM. The sex is fabulous, inventive and orgasmic moments that will touch your heart and leave you breathless." ~ *Just Erotic Romance Review.*

Scarlet Cavern

Vonna Harper

SCARLET CAVERN
An Ellora's Cave Publication, April 2005

Ellora's Cave Publishing, Inc.
1337 Commerce Drive, Suite #13
Stow, Ohio 44224

ISBN # 1419951866

Edited by: *Martha Punches*
Cover art by: *Syneca*

Warning:

Also by Vonna Harper:

Scarlet Cavern

Prologue

"Are you alone?" sixteen-year-old Shana Galliher asked the girl on the other end of the phone line.

"Yeah. He left for work, finally."

Shana sat up, no longer half asleep. "What about your mom?"

"Who knows? She and what's-his-face had a fight earlier. When she took off, she said she didn't know when she'd be back."

"And she left you with him?"

"Yeah."

"Are you all right?"

Lindsay, who was Shana's best friend and dream-sharer, didn't immediately answer. "Sure," Lindsay said at length, her tone unconvincing. "Why shouldn't I be? After all, we both know the drill. Besides, he said he'd buy me a new outfit."

In exchange for molesting you. Shana glanced at the clock in her bedroom, a little after 11 p.m. on a school night, not that it mattered. "I'm coming over," she said.

"No! I mean, I didn't call because I wanted to cry on your shoulder. I just thought, well…"

You don't cry, not anymore. "My folks are out of town," Shana said. "I told you about Grandma's surgery, didn't I? They're going to be gone at least until the weekend."

"I'm a big girl. I can take care of myself. I just—look, I

don't know why I'm bothering you, all right."

"That's what best friends do," Shana explained. Slipping out of bed, she reached for the clothes she'd been wearing earlier, not bothering with underwear. "Look, neither of us is going to be able to sleep now, right?"

Lindsay didn't answer, but her shaky sigh reached across the three miles separating them.

"Hang tight," Shana said. "I'll be right there."

Not giving Lindsay time to try to talk her out of it, she hung up the phone. Fortunately, her parents had made good on their promise to buy her a car as long as she kept her grades up. Although it would never win any beauty contests and could barely keep up in a race with a bicycle, the car was reliable transportation and a lot safer than walking. The trip should be enough for her to plan what she needed to say to Lindsay, shouldn't it? What she needed to do.

* * * * *

No, it wasn't, Shana acknowledged as she pulled into the dirt driveway of the little rental Lindsay lived in with her mom and her mother's latest boyfriend, a man who creeped her out whenever she was in the same room with him. He never looked her in the eye. Instead, his disgusting gaze said he wanted to get his hands on her C-cup breasts.

Lindsay was sitting on the dinky front porch in her faded nightgown, her feet on the top step, arms locked around her bent knees as if trying to hug herself. Thanks to the army of moths around the dim bulb, Shana couldn't read Lindsay's expression like she needed to.

What could she possibly say to the girl she considered

her sister, a girl who shared her love of track and science, a girl who couldn't remember her father and knew there'd never be the money for college?

"You want to blow this town?" Shana asked as she sat next to the shivering Lindsay. "We could pack our bathing suits and get on the next plane for Hawaii. Spend the next month on the beach getting tanned and staring at male surfers."

"I don't want anything to do with boys."

For a moment, Shana let the words hang. She couldn't imagine not being interested in boys. In truth, for the past year or so it had been darn hard to think of anything else, and if Jeff didn't ask her to the prom...

Knock it off! This isn't about Jeff or you.

"Do you want to talk about it?" she asked. She wanted to suggest they go inside, but she hated being in the tiny, crowded, dirty place and knew it was even worse for Lindsay.

"No."

Because she'd expected that, she simply shrugged. "Was it the same as the last time?" she prodded. "He'd been drinking?"

"What does it matter!" Lindsay snapped. Then she sighed and shook her head. "I'm sorry. I'm not mad at you."

"I know you aren't."

"It's me." Lindsay leaned forward and covered her face with her hands. "I should know how to stop him. Fight. Something."

"He's huge and with that belly—"

"I'm faster than him. But when he comes after me, I

11

get so scared." She took a shaky breath. "I hate being scared and feeling dirty. Hate everything about...*it.*"

It was rape, and she and Lindsay knew that. "I, ah, was it like before when he, you know, put his *thing* in your mouth?"

"No," Lindsay admitted with her face still in her hands. "The last time he couldn't get it up, but this time he — you don't want to hear this."

No, I don't. But I think you need to say it. "Lindsay, you can't keep it bottled up inside you. So, so he got an erection. What-what did he do with it?"

"Put it in me."

"What?" The moment the word was out of her mouth, she couldn't believe she'd said something so stupid.

"Made me lie on the floor with my legs spread while he — it hurt."

"Bad?"

"Not like the first time."

Despite her revulsion, Shana struggled to comprehend what *it* had felt like. She was a virgin although Jeff and a couple of other guys had been trying to talk her out of the status for months now, and she was giving it serious consideration. She'd taken the health classes, gotten *the* talk from her mother, seen enough R-rated movies to know what sex was like.

But rape and sex weren't the same thing; her mother had made it clear that no man had a right to force her to do something she didn't want to. And what's-his-face had been forcing Lindsay since shortly after he'd moved in right after Christmas. Sex was supposed to be great, right? Just thinking about having Jeff's fingers and penis between her legs turned her cheeks hot, but if some fat drunk man was doing it, she'd barf.

"Talk to Mrs. Albers," she said, referring to their track coach. "She meant it when she said she was there for anything. Or the police. They'd—"

"No!" Lindsay scrambled to her feet and started pacing. "No! And you can't say anything either."

"He's breaking the law."

"I don't want anyone to know, to have to tell…"

"You told me."

"You're different."

"You have to let someone know and who better than me? We tell each other everything, right? Lindsay, I can't stand not doing anything."

"I'll get him to stop." Lindsay sounded desperate. In the inadequate light, her face looked bloodless. "I will. The next time he comes near me, I'll scream and kick him where it'll do the most good."

With everything in her, Shana wanted to believe Lindsay. But although her friend was the school's fastest female sprinter and hadn't gotten below an A in any science class, she had little self-confidence. Shana believed she knew why. With a father who didn't seem to care whether she was alive, a mother who acted like it was Lindsay's fault she'd been born, and four older siblings who'd cut and run the moment they turned eighteen, how was Lindsay supposed to feel worthwhile?

Sometimes—rarely—Shana wished she'd chosen someone who didn't live from crisis to crisis as her best friend, but Lindsay needed her.

Lindsay knew things about her she'd never told anyone, like her dreams of becoming a model because

Lindsay understood dreams and secrets and caring.

And that made them close, bonded.

"Come home with me," she finally came up with. "You can leave your mother a note."

"Your parents—"

"Are out of town. Besides, they love you."

"They wouldn't if they knew." Lindsay stepped close. "You haven't said anything, have you? You promised you wouldn't."

"No, I haven't," Shana admitted. Not for the first time, she hated herself for agreeing to silence when she should be raising heaven and earth getting Lindsay out of this nightmare. Some day, when she was older and in control, she'd become Lindsay's savior.

Somehow.

It was a promise.

Chapter One
Fifteen years later

Shana stepped inside the nondescript door and reluctantly closed it behind her. The interior was too dark and quiet. Her every instinct screamed at her to return to the successful, in-control life she'd carved for herself, but of course she couldn't.

Until she'd learned whether Lindsay was dead or alive, nothing else mattered.

When her eyes adjusted to the gloom, she realized she was in a long, narrow hall. Recovery should have—what—certainly a more impressive looking office. She'd been led to believe the private organization had connections that put the FBI and Secret Service to shame, but she had her doubts. Shit, it had cost her a thousand dollars just to get enough information about Recovery to understand the organization dedicated itself to doing whatever it took to help people regain something or someone they'd lost. Their methods weren't always legal but apparently they refused to do anything that would put anyone's life at risk. If the head of security for a precious gems company had lied to her, she'd—what, sue the man while maybe Lindsay's life lay in the balance?

Thoughts of what might have happened to the woman she still considered her sister sent Shana down the hall. In the years since she and Lindsay had shared everything, she'd turned her body into a finely honed tool and become the model she'd dreamed of back when

Lindsay was living a nightmare. Most times she accepted her body as her meal ticket, but today she was grateful for her muscular legs, the product of endless hours in the gym and running track. If she didn't like what she saw about Recovery, she'd turn tail and run.

Only she couldn't.

Are you still alive, Lindsay? Please, you have to be!

The sign on the door at the end of the hall looked as if it had been nailed up by someone who'd never used a hammer before, but when she depressed the latch, she noted the door was steel. There were two deadbolts. As she stepped inside, she caught a humming sound. A bank of glowing monitors on a far wall explained a lot about the sound. Whoever was behind the San Diego branch of Recovery relied on high-tech.

At first glance, the room looked empty, but that was because it was so large that taking it all in took time. There were several cubicles, each with its own computer. Intense, casually dressed men and women hunched over the units.

A thin middle-aged woman stood and walked toward her, her gaze never leaving Shana. "You're looking for Galen, right?" she said.

"I—yes, that's the name I was given. But before I see him, could you tell me more about what happens here?"

"There isn't much I can say because we're dedicated to our clients' privacy, but we do things people can't on their own like—for example, we just helped a man set up a trust for the daughter he hadn't seen since she was an infant. He couldn't find her on his own. Now they're starting to build a relationship."

"It sounds wonderful."

"Sometimes it is. Other times — there." The woman pointed at a room to the left. "He's expecting you."

"Oh," Shana managed. She didn't know what she'd expected, maybe armed guards, maybe being frisked, something. Instead, no one seemed concerned that an outsider had walked into the middle of things. Then she realized everyone was watching her.

Could they feel her tension, her fear, the undeniable sexual excitement spawned by the unknown?

Turned on? Shit, Shana, are you insane?!

Pretending indifference, she thanked the woman. Like the first one, this door was substantial, nearly impenetrable. This new room was maybe a tenth the size of the outer one and consisted of a large cluttered desk with several well-worn easy chairs clustered around it. Behind the desk, nearly obscured by it, sat a man who couldn't have been more than five and a half feet tall. Like the woman out front, he'd said goodbye to his forties, and like the woman, his gaze locked on her. She was used to drawing attention and most times took it for what it was worth which wasn't much. But right now wasn't about her. Only Lindsay mattered.

The man had almost no hair and from its straggly appearance, he couldn't care less. His shirt looked as if he'd pulled it out of the dryer after it had sat there for days. His hands were large compared to the rest of him, and when he stood and came around the desk toward her, she wondered when he'd last bothered to eat.

"I'm Galen," he said, holding out his hand. "And you're Shana."

"Yes." He hadn't invited her to sit down so she continued to stand. The room smelled of old wood and dust, yet his computer setup looked as if a person could run the space program from it.

"All right, Shana, I know you have a lot of questions about Recovery, but first I want to give you an idea of how efficient we are. If you don't mind, I'd like to bring the operative you'll be working with in now."

The operative? Like a human being?

Before she could decide whether to make a point of the odd term, the door she'd just come through opened again, and a man filled the space. Hell, he did more than fill it, he commanded it.

His height? Well over six feet and as hard as a seasoned professional athlete. The black and silver Oakland Raiders logo T-shirt he wore seemed painted on muscle and bone. For a moment she couldn't take her eyes off the pirate figure in the middle of his chest. Was the man encased in the shirt the embodiment of the pirate, savage and aggressive—taker of things or people he desired?

An icy fist gripped her heart, making it hard to breathe. At the same time, she felt rawly alive. With an effort, she continued her appraisal. He stood with his legs slightly spread, impressive chest muscles forcing his arms out a bit from his body. He needed a shave. Surely once he'd run a razor over his chin he'd look less dark, less shadowed. Surely. He also needed a haircut although the unkempt length added to the uncivilized male look. His eyes were coal-black, deep-set and large, penetrating.

Suddenly scared, Shana forced her attention off the big, dark, maybe deadly male.

"Shana," Galen said. "This is Ranger."

Ranger? Doesn't he have a last name?

Shaking hands with Galen had been easy but no way in hell was she ready to let this-this animal-like creature touch her. She managed a nod at the still-silent man and sank into the nearest chair. She couldn't begin to relax. "What do you mean, operative?" she asked. Damn, her voice held a husky note, the voice of a woman turned on.

Galen looked at Ranger, obviously waiting for him to answer her question. When Ranger only continued his predator-like perusal of her, Galen sighed. "The website you directed us to when you first contacted Recovery — the Scarlet Cavern — how much do you know about it?"

For an instant, all air seemed to leave the room. *This is important,* she thought. *Maybe the most important thing you'll do in your life. Life-changing.*

"Not much," she admitted in that sex-deepened tone. "Just what I saw from the public pages."

"Which are practically useless." Ranger spoke for the first time, his voice low and rough. "What's there gets past the morality patrol. Only those who have been allowed access get the real picture."

"And you have access?" she asked, cold again.

He nodded.

"In what context?" she demanded. When he only returned her stare, she switched her attention to Galen who struck her as being tenser than he'd been at the beginning. "All right, so all I have are the teasers to go by." She suppressed a shudder. "But what I saw — the short movie clips of my best friend being beaten — naked, tied and gagged..." She took a deep breath. "How much worse can it get?"

"Enough," Ranger muttered. He stepped all the way in the room and leaned against Galen's desk. He'd positioned himself, maybe deliberately, so his cock was nearly at her eye level. *Ignore that* he seemed to be saying.

This isn't going to work! I can't — on the verge of blurting she'd made a terrible mistake and didn't want to know any more than she did about the perverted world of Scarlet Cavern, a single image from the clips of Lindsay burst to the forefront. Despite the video's jerky quality, she'd seen several whip blows strike Lindsay's breasts. Someone had fastened metal clamps to Lindsay's nipples and each blow had caused them to jerk. She'd had nightmares about the awful sound of strips of leather striking flesh and Lindsay's moans under the leather gag. The worst had come when the camera panned up to Lindsay's face. Her eyes had been huge and helpless. Alive.

What's happened to you? Is this the only reason you stopped being in touch? I thought — hell, I don't know what I thought — anything except this.

"All right." She forced emotion out of her voice. "So you have access to the site's inner contents. How does one join? I-I tried but was rejected. Something about needing to be recommended by a current member."

"You tried?" Ranger cocked his head at her. "Why?"

"Not because pictures of abused women turn me on, that's for damn sure!" she retorted. No one need ever know she'd been sitting at the computer with her pink plastic clit teaser on high while exploring what the search engine had on bondage because she'd long been curious about the lifestyle — if that's what it was called — when she'd stumbled across Scarlet Cavern — and Lindsay. "Look, if it had been you accidentally coming across an explicit sex site and finding your best friend being exploited — "

"Best friend? If you're that close, how come you didn't know what she was up to?"

"Up to? It's hardly the same as going on vacation. We're close, always have been. It's just that — you know — each living our own lives." *Mine being a lot more organized than hers and maybe her feeling as if she wasn't measuring up and me feeling — shit — maybe feeling superior and irritated with her lack of direction.* "I hadn't seen or talked to her for about three months. I didn't realize it had been that long until I started thinking about it."

"What were you doing exploring such sites?"

Damn him! Damn him! "Curiosity."

His mouth twitched.

"I don't owe you any more of an explanation," she retorted. "I'm free, white, and over twenty-one."

"Ranger." Galen's voice held a warning note. "The how and why of her getting there are unimportant."

"Maybe." His gaze had held on her face since he'd entered the room, but now his eyes trailed lower. She felt his heat on her throat, breasts, belly, between her legs. "And you believe your friend isn't there of her own free will?"

Just like that, everything else — even the hot message in his study of her — became unimportant. She leaned forward, one hand at her throat. "Impossible. Lindsay and I have shared everything since elementary school. I had the stereotypical middle-class upbringing complete with stay-at-home mom and white-collar father. They're still married, still in love with each other. I have two older brothers both happily married with children."

"Unlike you. You're still single."

How much do they know about me? "Yes, I'm single."

"Without a steady boyfriend because you've put your career first. You're making an unreal amount of money modeling and promoting exercise clothing, but you know your years of banking on your physical body are limited so you're investing in the company you work for. At the same time, you're designing high school girls' running shoes and plan to present them to major athletic shoe companies."

Oh God. "You've done your homework," she acknowledged. "I'd ask how you learned those things, but you wouldn't tell me, would you?"

"No."

"Why not?"

Galen sighed. "Shana, you probably don't know this, but you're asking Recovery and specifically Ranger to undertake a complex operation. Scarlet Cavern has been in existence for many years and has extensive contacts, many powerful, wealthy, and influential members who are determined to retain their anonymity. My first responsibility to my operative—" he paused and jerked his head at Ranger, "is to guarantee his safety. You check out. You have no connection to political or business foes of any Scarlet Cavern members."

This was getting way too complex. All she cared about was saving her friend, if it wasn't already too late. Prompted by the knot of fear for the woman she considered her sister, she stood and leaned over Galen's desk. Doing so placed her within inches of Ranger. "Do you know as much about Lindsay as you do about me?" she asked.

"No," Galen admitted, "because until you mentioned her name a few minutes ago, we didn't know who you wanted to find."

"You still don't know her." Shana glanced at Ranger. Damn, did he have to be so tall, so imposing? And what was with the sexuality oozing from his pores? A woman would have to be dead not to feel it and she wasn't dead—far from it.

"Tell us," Ranger said. The order rumbled from him, and she felt the vibration everywhere, mostly between her legs.

Lindsay, this is for you. Otherwise—otherwise I'd be running from this man. Either that or jumping his bones. "Lindsay's father walked out when she was a baby. Her mother was—is—a beautiful but insecure woman. She can't live without a man and works at her one drawing card, her looks. Unfortunately, she has lousy taste in the opposite sex."

Ranger's expression changed. *Get to the point*, it said.

"You've heard the jokes about children who grow up with a succession of *uncles*? That's what happened to my best friend. And some of them, particularly a building contractor who was around for much of her teenage years, believed the daughter came with the mother."

"He molested Lindsay?"

"Yes," she managed. "Over and over again until—until I told my parents, and my father had him arrested."

"How did Lindsay handle it?" Ranger asked, showing something that might be emotion for the first time.

"Scared, grateful." *And until I told her everything, so angry at me I thought I'd ruined everything between us.* "Her-her mother didn't believe her at first. Lindsay had to testify against Jake." She took a hopefully calming breath. "So did I. Testimony from two girls with no reason to lie resulted in a conviction."

Something brushed the back of her hand. Startled, Shana looked down. Ranger's hand rested a bare inch from hers. Had it been a comforting gesture on his part?

"Jake got to you, too?" Galen asked.

She swallowed. "Yes. But only twice, not the way he bothered Lindsay." *All he did was take my virginity.* Knowing she'd never tell these men that, she straightened. "Gentlemen, Lindsay and I have been through a great deal together. We had to testify in court and before that—I don't know if you can understand this, but I know things about Lindsay—having to do with her introduction to sex and her current feelings about her sexuality... Scarlet Cavern touts itself as a gathering place for *consenting* adults committed to exercise their legal rights to explore and test the limits of domination and submission." She'd memorized Scarlet Cavern's motto, not because she'd ever embrace the lifestyle—surely not—but because she'd needed to understand the world Lindsay had been forced into.

"After what Lindsay went through with Jake and a couple of other so-called uncles, she'd never willingly place herself in a submissive relationship. Being in control is vital to her survival. That's why she's always been self-employed, doing everything from house-sitting to designing and building award-winning landscape ponds. What I saw in those clips—" Bile rose in her throat, but she forced it down. "I'll never believe that shit about consent. Lindsay is being held against her will. She's—what do they call it?—a white slave? Whatever it takes, whatever I have to do, I'm going to get her out of there."

Unless it's too late.

Chapter Two

"I've changed my mind," Galen said. "I don't want you working with her after all."

Because he'd known Galen would say that, Ranger had no reaction. His mind, hell, his body, remained locked on the woman who'd just left. A predator—and he was one—could always sense prey. She'd probably rip out his eyes if he told her he'd started hunting and wouldn't stop until he brought her down. At least she'd fight if he gave her the chance—which he wouldn't. *Wouldn't! Past tense.*

And yet old habits and desires died hard.

"Did you hear me?" Galen insisted. "I'm assigning her to another operative."

"No, you're not."

"Damn it, I pay your—"

"I'll quit." Ranger paced to the window and looked out at the parking lot. Shana left the building's shadows and walked toward her virgin-white sports car. The car amused him because she was no virgin. She was too alive, too sexual a creature to have anything in common with the word. Why the smokescreen the automobile represented, he pondered. Then as her long, lean legs ate up the yards, he found the answer. *Because she doesn't know how to handle her hunger, her sensuality.*

"I'm the only one who can do this," he told the older man. "We both know it."

"Damn it."

"Yeah, damn it." He could point out that no one else had complete access to Scarlet Cavern but Galen already knew it. "She's willing to pay an obscene amount of money. I want this job. I just wrapped up my last one and need to stay employed."

"You don't give a damn about or need more money. And you don't care what the Cavern people do, so—"

"I do if they're abusing someone."

"This is what this is about? You haven't gotten over what happened there. The guilty were prosecuted. You did your job."

"Did I?" He made no attempt to keep bitterness out of his voice. "Two abusers are in prison, but a woman is still dead."

"You can't save the world, Ranger. Hell, the two of us together can't begin to make a dent."

Galen was right. Didn't he know all too well the power and seduction of the dark side? Given the right circumstances, hell, given the right woman's body under his control, and he might never again escape what had always held his father in its grip. Just looking at Shana had awakened his baser nature and sent his imagination into overdrive. He'd loved the hunt, the game, the feeling of power and the sounds and smells of a woman's surrender. But he'd spent the past three years fighting the devil. He could do it. He *had* to.

"Are you listening?" Galen demanded. "Damn it, Ranger, when I'm working with you I feel like I've got a junkyard dog at the end of a short leash. As long as I keep him under control, that dog will keep my property safe, but if he gets loose—"

"I won't go for your throat."

"Maybe." Galen stared at him as if expecting him to grow fangs. "But I know what you're capable of, what you've done."

"It's the past," Ranger insisted even as his history's seductive fingers stroked him. "You heard her. She doesn't believe her friend is in the Cavern under her own free will. If this Lindsay is being abused, I've got to get her out of there."

Galen nodded, his features somber. "I agree. The thing is, will you come out with Lindsay or stay this time?" He paused. "And what about Shana? Will you take her in with you?"

"I have to. She won't accept anything else."

"Answer my question. Will you come out?"

"I'm damned if I don't."

"Maybe you don't mind hell."

* * * * *

Ranger had said he'd get in touch with her. She was supposed to wait for him, plan things so she could be away from work for a week or more, understand that when he showed up, his means and methods would mirror Lindsay's experience.

"What the hell did you mean?" Shana demanded of the air at the end of a long and stressful day. She'd gone straight to her office after leaving Recovery and had spent the next ten hours tying up loose ends. Now, tired and hungry, she wanted only two things in life—food and answers.

Make that three things, she admitted as she trudged through the ill-lit and nearly empty parking garage to her car. Wrung out as she was, a part of her still hadn't been able to shake off Ranger's impact.

He was more than a stud, more than macho man. He was—what—as seductive and dangerous as a burning candle, a blazing structure. If she'd ever met a more nakedly sexual man she couldn't remember—and she would, wouldn't she?

Watch it, Shana. You don't know him, and you sure as hell don't trust him.

No, I don't. But it doesn't matter; I want him.

She stopped, designer purse clutched to her side. A moment ago she'd been debating kicking off her heels and going barefoot, wanting to dig into her purse for something to counter her headache, needing to close her eyes and rest them.

Now only one thing mattered. The female animal in her wanted to mate with the male animal known as Ranger. Despite her traumatic introduction, she loved sex, the seduction and striptease, the sweat and screaming climax. Yes, in the aftermath of fucking she always experienced a measure of self-fear because she had so little control over what she did when she was turned on, but even in the light of day, she knew she'd fuck again. She had no choice! Her body—hell, her soul—craved those moments when her muscles and nerves and bones exploded.

And Ranger could make her explode in ways she'd never experienced.

Make? As in force a climax?

Unnerved, she closed in on her car. Her blood sugar must be low. A bite of something sweet and she'd regain her equilibrium. The damn sexy man would stop tromping around in her brain and on her nerve endings and between her legs. She'd stop fantasizing about what he looked like naked.

Movement just beyond her car caused her heart to race. She reached into her purse for the canister of mace she always carried. Her car stood alone in a row of parking slots. True, there were a couple of SUVs nearby and a Lexus in the next row, but they did precious little to take away her sense of isolation and vulnerability.

"Who is it?" she asked. Her shaky tone gave away too much. "Who's out there?"

"Good instincts," Ranger said and stepped out of the shadows. He stood near her front bumper. He appeared to be dressed all in black, a hunting panther. "You're aware of your surroundings," he added.

He's testing you. "Thanks for the compliment, if that's what it is."

"It's an observation. Are you ready? You haven't changed your mind about turning your life over to me?"

"Are you trying to scare me?"

"I probably will, but if I do things right, before long you'll understand how seductive the *lifestyle* is. I'll repeat myself. You're in this for the long run? Mine to manage until you say enough?"

"You mean I can walk away whenever I want?"

"I wouldn't have it any other way."

Are you brave enough for this, she read in his words. *Do you have what it takes?* "Let's get started."

He nodded and gave her what might pass as a smile for him. She was waiting for the smile to expand when he launched himself at her. He easily wrapped his arms around her and pinned her arms to her side. At the same

29

moment, he spun her toward her car hood and forced her to lean over it. He released her arms but held her head against the cold metal, her cheek flattened on the surface.

She tried to straighten. He shifted position, and she felt his forearm press into the back of her neck. Despite her frantic struggle, he easily captured one wrist and pulled it up and back in what felt like a practiced gesture. Using his hold for leverage, he kept her against the car while he snagged her other wrist and crossed it over the first. Her shoulders burned. She couldn't lift her head enough to let out a scream. A horrifying clicking sound accompanied by the feel of steel over her wrists left no doubt. He'd handcuffed her.

With her arms immobile, he grabbed her shoulders and yanked her into an upright position. She opened her mouth to scream. Cloth was shoved into it followed by tape being wrapped around her head to keep the cloth in place. At least he had the courtesy to lift her hair off her neck first.

"There," he announced. "Step one, minimize resistance."

Her every nerve felt on fire. It took incredible effort to look into his eyes. Night shrouded his features and made him appear deadly — powerful.

"I'll explain how the Scarlet Cavern operates as we go through your introduction." His tone was conversational. "The line between play and reality has a way of blurring, particularly at the beginning. This isn't the same as a modeling shoot with props, cameras and makeup people, agents and clients or whatever the hell you have. This is you and me. You're going to have a thousand questions and doubts, but for you to fully experience what your friend went through, you need to walk in her footsteps."

What are you talking about? What are you doing?

"Because you agreed to it, starting tonight your world has changed," he said, still holding her hair. "Everything will be revealed as we progress, but it will happen slowly as I introduce you to a world you don't yet know exists — one your friend may have embraced."

No! She can't want what I saw happening to her!

"I will make you one promise, Shana." He pulled on her long straight hair, bringing her so close his features blurred. "You will get out of this alive. Your life is not in danger. And if at any time you can't handle it, say the word."

Despite his reassuring comment, fear weakened her muscles. She'd never been restrained or silenced in her life. Oh, true, she fantasized about being captured by some powerful man — the accompanying images had proven to be a sure route to a quick, easy, and wild climax and explained why she'd been surfing bondage sites when she found Lindsay. But this was no mind or visual game to be indulged in when she had nothing except her vibrator to keep her company.

"This is hardly the place to begin your education," he said, nodding to indicate the other cars. "Privacy comes first." Still controlling her via the grip on her hair, he leaned down and picked up the purse she'd dropped. He placed it on the car hood and dug through it, grunting when he found her keys. He punched the remote, unlocking her doors.

"I don't suppose you've ever been in the backseat," he observed. "A business woman like yourself, you don't believe in a quickie back there. However, that's where you're going tonight."

He shoved her toward it. The dark interior reminded her of a cave and slammed her up against the reality that once he had her in it, he could take her wherever he wanted. Sobbing under the gag, she kicked him. At least she tried. Unfortunately, her heels found nothing except air.

"So that's what I have, a fighter." He snagged her elbows and pushed her face first onto the seat with her legs still outside. Because her hands were behind her, she lacked the leverage to lift herself off the leather. A shaky breath brought the scent of leather into her nostrils. The smell was heady, warm, and could it be, calming? Before she could decide, he captured her ankles and folded her legs up so her heels touched her ass.

Using the power and expertise she'd already come to expect, he wrapped lengths of tape around her ankles so her legs were lashed together. Not content with that, he used more of the seemingly endless tape to bind her ankles and wrists together, hogtieing her.

"Not comfortable, I know." He patted her ass almost tenderly. "I'm sorry about that, but I don't want you kicking the windows and drawing attention to us. Besides—" He squeezed her right ass cheek. "Getting used to helplessness is the first step."

What first step? Oh please, what are you doing?!

He repositioned her so she lay on her side then got behind the steering wheel. After pushing the seat all the way back to accommodate his size, he started the engine. The cloth in her mouth made her half-sick, but that was nothing compared to her fear.

Fear. The word and accompanying sensations rolled over her in waves as he exited the parking garage. He turned in the opposite direction of her condo, unnerving her even more. He'd said she'd come out of this alive and could pull the plug if she wanted, and she wanted to believe him — God, did she! He'd also intimated that he intended to duplicate her best friend's experience, but she could barely comprehend that Lindsay had undergone the same helplessness, the same unease.

And yet...

The car picked up speed, and although she didn't want it, she found herself being lulled by the smooth motor sounds. Being tied up was hardly comfortable, but she'd given the mysterious Recovery an advance payment to help her find Lindsay, and the only way they'd get the rest of the considerable sum she'd agreed to was by putting her in touch with her friend. Surely Galen wouldn't have turned her over to a madman — would he?

The cuffs rubbed against her wrists, but she didn't think they would leave marks. Because he'd used tape on her ankles, all she felt there was confinement. Not being able to speak sucked big time and as for the hogtie, well...

Well, there was something sexy about being this man's prisoner.

Are you insane? You can't possibly mean this?

What if he insisted on keeping her for a while?

Keeping her? Hot and cold by turn, she shifted position and looked up at the back of his head. This wasn't a game, was it? He intended to — what?

Heat flowed into her pussy, and she grew wet. This wasn't simple sexual excitement. In a moment she'd been ripped out of her comfortable world, stripped of all control over her own body. It — and she — belonged to him for as long as she chose.

* * * * *

Ranger pulled into the drive leading to the hilltop house belonging to Scarlet Cavern, a place he'd once considered his and still had access to. Although he could have activated the garage opener, he wanted Shana to see enough of their surroundings to understand how isolated the place was. After getting out, he opened the rear door and pushed her onto her belly again so he could release the tape holding her legs against her body. He'd told himself to take things slow, to introduce her to the concept of being his prisoner before introducing other elements, but he ran his hands up her skirt and kneaded her ass.

She felt hot, alive, woman! And he was, under the layers, a junkyard dog, a predator who'd just captured fresh prey. She squirmed, muttered something intelligible, and tried to kick. Deftly avoiding her feet, he pulled her pantyhose and underpants down around her knees. Then he freed her ankles and yanked her out and onto her feet. She tried to stumble away, but the makeshift knee tether hobbled her. He gripped her upper arms and began steering her toward the front porch, going slow so she wouldn't lose her balance, and to give her time to take in her surroundings.

"Take a good look around," he told her. "Get used to the idea of being out of your element and in a remote area." The house, part of an exclusive community, came with a couple of acres of land.

Among the improvements current Scarlet Cavern management had made was an extensive security system. When activated, no one could come or leave without the system announcing his or her intentions. Not even a window could be opened without the appropriate code. In addition, the windows were one-way, allowing guests to see out but making it impossible for the curious to see in. Two rooms had been fitted with sound-deadening material, and the doors to them locked from the outside.

"Take a look, Shana," he told her. "Note the trees, the fencing. You couldn't see it of course, but we came in through a gate that I've locked behind me. This isn't the main Scarlet Cavern complex but a private place used for a multitude of purposes. I checked; no one will be using it for the next few days. We're secure here, isolated."

She looked up at him, her eyes big and bright. He had no doubt of her fear, but he sensed more. She was turned on. Hell, he, who'd honed his skill in all things sexual, could smell her.

Maybe she belonged in the world he'd once embraced and still called to him.

When they reached the door, he released her and put the key in the lock. As he suspected, she tried to back away. The fabric around her knees stopped her, and she might have lost her balance if he hadn't snagged her again, this time around the waist.

"Not going to happen, Shana," he warned as he half-pushed, half-carried her into the house. "Your training has begun."

He flipped on a switch, activating the three lamps in the large living room and casting the space in soft light. To his mind, the off-white carpeting and white leather furniture was a bit much, but he guessed it went with the massive marble fireplace.

Closing the door behind him had taken him back in time to when he'd surrounded himself with black, not white, when he'd been part of the Cavern and everything it stood for. He was like an old warrior, no longer allowed to fight but with the instinct still running hot through him.

No matter. He knew his job. He'd do it somehow.

"It'll all be explained to you in due time. Eventually you'll understand everything, but it has to come by degrees. Otherwise you'll never understand what happened to your friend."

She gave him another of those uncomprehending looks, and he fought the urge—hell, the need—to throw her to the floor, rip off her pantyhose and bury himself in her. But he didn't rape. He'd never rape.

"It's late. You haven't eaten, have you?" he asked.

After a moment she shook her head.

"We'll get to that eventually. The lessons begin tonight, and you'll want to stay strong."

She seemed to shrink into herself, then straightened. The determination in her eyes might have had more impact if she didn't have tape over her mouth and her arms cuffed behind her. He was glad to see her fire. It would change over time and become something she didn't now comprehend, but the glare reinforced what he believed about her. She was strong. Her strength would make changing her more of a challenge, but he fed off challenge—especially one issued by a woman's body. He could be wrong of course, but he didn't see her as a quitter. She'd see this through to the end, and they'd feed off each other.

Feeling a little like a tour guide, he took her through the whole house, keeping the room he'd intended for her until last. The place boasted four bedrooms and three baths, a state of the art kitchen, dining room, and breakfast nook. Most impressive was the den overlooking the wooded acreage. One wall was all double-strength windows, affording those who sat in the high-end recliners and couches a spectacular view of unspoiled land.

"You'll spend some time in here," he assured her. "Not yet, but when I say you can. For now, let's get you settled into the room I've reserved for you."

He pushed her ahead of him, deliberately going fast so she had to struggle to stay on her feet.

He opened the metal door to what was sarcastically called the lab but didn't turn on the light. Going by memory, he brought his *prisoner* to the middle of the room. He knelt, found the bolt driven into the floor and took hold of the chain and ankle cuffs attached to the bolt but didn't put them on her. Instead, he ran the chain over her ankles so she'd know what he had in mind. She sobbed again, the sound less angry than before. She didn't try to run, and he respected her self-control at the same time he acknowledged yet another sign of her untapped dark side.

"Remember, what you're going through is a process, an option," he informed her. "We're walking a fine line between consent and coercion."

After a moment she nodded. He closed his fingers over hose and panties and began peeling the nylon down. He stopped when they were around her ankles, struggled against the junkyard dog in him, surrendered.

After clamping a hand around her buttocks so she couldn't get away, he ran the other up between her legs. She tried to twist one way and the other but only managed to lose her balance. He helped her regain it.

"You don't want to make that mistake again," he said. "All you'll accomplish by falling is bruising yourself."

She took a miniscule backward step, then stopped, the

nylon ankle restraints doing their job. He gave her a moment to get used to his hands, then started exploring her pussy, branding it and letting her know she'd become his. She clamped her legs together which only increased his determination. Ignoring the pressure on his hand and forearm, he reached with thumb and forefinger. Finding her cunt lips, he gently rubbed the sleek, soft flesh. Her thigh muscles relaxed slightly. He took one lip between thumb and finger and drew down on it. A woman's labia was a beautiful thing, intoxicating. He loved the smell of sex juice, the texture and taste of it. He, whose life revolved around maintaining control, felt weak in the face of his need to fuck.

He might have temporary mastery of Shana's body, but the real power lay between her legs. And if she ever put her arms around him and pressed her mouth against his, everything would shift to her. He *had* to prevent that from happening, had to remain the one on top in more ways than one because if he didn't—if he ever let a woman into his soul…

Angry at both of them, he ran his forefinger inside her as far as it would go. She cursed into the gag but other than a slight shudder, didn't move. His finger was immediately drenched in liquid heat, and he pictured her cunt turning red and swollen. He remained housed in her, as still as she was, getting to know her, reacquainting himself with a woman's cave and the strength that went with it.

He wanted, not his hand invading her sex, but his cock buried deep and hard and urgent. His cock, already erect, became even more engorged. Despite the discomfort caused by the confining fabric of his jeans, he wasn't distracted from the treasure he'd found. He opened his mouth but didn't speak because he had nothing to say — or rather anything he said would reveal too much.

She was a client, their arrangement financial. True, her request of Recovery would take them into a sensual and sometimes dangerous world, but she'd signed a contract and given the agency money and given him permission to take control of her body, and he had a responsibility to fulfill the terms of that contract.

Nothing else.

Hell, he hadn't come close to comprehending her devotion to the woman who'd brought them together.

Fighting old and persistent demons, he withdrew his finger, wiping it on her inner thigh.

"Think about the wet," he whispered. "It's the bottom line, Shana. Everything that happened to your friend and what you're going to go through boils down to this one thing." He pulled off her hose and panties one leg at a time. Then he did the same with her skirt and fastened the metal ankle restraints in place. "Underneath it all, a woman is a primitive creature. When all is said and done, only sex matters, right?"

She blinked repeatedly and started to shake her head. Then, teeth clenched, she nodded.

"We're on the same page, are we? Giving and accepting certain lessons?"

After another nod, she shifted her weight as she experimented with her new tethers. Taking advantage of her distraction, he unfastened her wrists then cuffed her arms in front of her.

"I'll be gone a few minutes," he informed her. He rammed his hands in his pockets to keep from touching her again. "In the meantime, why don't you get as comfortable as possible."

Chapter Three

Shana waited until she could no longer hear his footsteps, then lifted her hands and touched the gag. It took awhile to get to what was at the back, but finally she pulled the last strip off her lips. Feeling proud of her accomplishment, she licked and nibbled until she'd removed most of the stickiness.

Because he'd left her in darkness, she knew nothing about the room and had only a vague understanding of what he'd put around her ankles. There were metal cuffs, so loose they didn't chafe her skin, and the chain between the cuffs was long enough that she could take a comfortable if careful step.

Bending down, she felt the restraint. When she discovered another chain affixed to the left cuff, she followed the coiled links to where it was attached to a bolt in the floor.

What was she, a chained dog?

No, a dog wouldn't — damn it — a dog wouldn't be turned on.

Disgusted with herself, she struggled to concentrate on the restraints and the things Ranger had done to her. Nothing in the contract she'd signed gave him the right to hold her against her will, and he'd repeatedly told her she could call an end to whatever this was whenever she wanted. Although she'd given him consent to *educate* her, she certainly hadn't given him permission to finger-fuck her.

Like she ever would!

Maybe.

*Lindsay, is this what happened to you? You experienced —
were you turned on when you became a Scarlet Cavern captive?
You told me you didn't care if you ever fucked a man after what
you'd been through, but is it possible bondage...*

Cold nibbled at her ass and thighs, reminding her that
she was naked from the waist down. He'd loved stripping
her; she knew he did! Without so much as a by-your-leave,
he'd rammed his hands between her legs and up into...

When had she stopped fighting the invasion and
allowed her baser nature to take over? All right, damn it,
she liked sex, liked it a lot! But always before she'd had it
on her terms. No way was a man ever going to use his
greater strength to force her to do something she didn't
want. If one tried — and in truth there'd only been two —
she'd plant a sharp knee where it got the most attention. In
her book, fucking was all about consent and mutual
respect. A dyed-in-the-wool women's libber, she'd always
hated that crap about the weaker sex. Weak, nothing! She-
she...

Weak? Maybe.

Maybe the faint metallic sounds of her chain had
snagged her attention. Maybe she'd finally allowed herself
to acknowledge her cuffed wrists. And maybe the truth lay
between her legs and the moisture he'd brought to life.

Overwhelmed with doubts and questions and a taste
of excitement and anticipation she could barely
acknowledge, she sank to her knees on the floor. Leaning
forward, she buried her face in her hands and began
rocking back and forth. She wasn't defeated. Far from it.

But she'd been through so much, subjected to *capture* and *degradation*. And her body had turned against her.

* * * * *

Shana closed her eyes against the sudden light. She'd heard the lock disengaging and had scrambled to her feet determined to confront Ranger, but damn it, she'd been in the dark so long it would take her eyes time to adjust. Certain he was using this as further proof of the upper hand he held, she refused to shrink from him.

Finally she focused on him. He stood just inside the opening, holding several items she didn't want to think about. Much as she needed to keep her eye on him, she also needed to learn more about her surroundings. The bolted-down four-poster bed with metal head and footboards standing in one corner did nothing to calm her nerves. Neither did the assortment of chains and leather restraints fastened to walls and the ceiling. There was a wooden dresser on legs with three drawers, a large recliner.

"You can't be serious," she managed.

"Yes I am. Shana, you're driven by a wish to rescue your friend, but you don't understand what you believe she needs rescuing from. For you to fully comprehend, you need to go through the same introduction she did."

"Introduction? Like she'd-she'd willingly agree to be whipped?"

He shrugged. "If you insist on semantics, what if we call it immersion?"

The word conjured up images of a dark, deep, cold body of water. A picture of her being forced into a lake with weights tied to her ankles overtook her. "She was kidnapped like me?" she managed.

"You really believe you've been kidnapped?"

"I don't know. Oh, all right; I have to believe I have been. It's the only way I can walk in her shoes."

"I agree which is why I did what I did to you. As for what happened to Lindsay, after a fashion she was taken against her will, although she gave out vibes that told the members of the Cavern she wanted the lifestyle."

It was too much to comprehend. Confused and overwhelmed, she stood with her cuffed hands over her exposed pubic hair, waiting.

"Ready?" he asked.

"I don't know."

"If you say you want out, it's the end to things. I'll take you to your place, and you'll never hear from me or anyone else at Recovery again. And I doubt if you'll ever know what happened to Lindsay."

Never know. My closest friend, lost.

She'd believed herself weak when she'd sunk to the floor in the dark, but that sensation was nothing compared to what now gripped her. "When-when I know everything and you've reunited me with Lindsay, you'll let me go and help her get free?"

"If she wants it. If you do."

What did he mean? Surely…

In silence comprehension, she lifted her manacled hands toward him. He studied her for a moment, his expression neutral. Then he clenched his jaw, tossed his assortment of chains and leather onto the bed, and stepped into her space.

"I won't tell you why I'm doing what I am, and you'll

never know what's coming, how long it'll last, or what you'll be like when it's over."

"You-you're scaring me." Her hands were so heavy she could barely hold them up.

"I intend to. From now we're operating in real time." He grabbed her left wrist and dragged her in that direction. The ankle chain got in the way, forcing her to concentrate on where she was going. Too late, she realized he'd lifted her hands over her head. A snapping sound startled her. He released her wrist, but when she tried to lower her arms, she found she couldn't. Looking up, she saw he'd hooked a length of chain fixed to the ceiling to her cuffs. Her hands were at head height, and she tugged.

"Don't bother," he said. "You aren't free until, or if, I want you to be."

Leaving her to digest that, he moved behind her. A moment later, she heard a grinding sound and felt her hands being pulled upward until she was practically on tiptoe. Looking behind her, she saw him working some kind of pulley.

"You're hurting—"

"No, I'm not. Not yet."

"What—?" she started to say. Before she could get another word out, he grabbed her hair and pulled her head back. She opened her mouth, and he shoved something in it. Outraged, she tried to spit it out, but he was too fast for her, locking the ball gag in place with a tight leather strap.

"Now you're caught inside yourself," he said as if explaining how to operate a tool. "Until I decide different, the communication is one-sided which is another way of saying there's no communication. One of the basic cannons of the Cavern is that the indoctrination takes place hard and fast. A subject off-balance has less opportunity to remain in emotional contact with the world she's always known." He covered her muff and gave it an almost companionable squeeze. "She's always trying to keep up with new stimuli."

His hand slid lower. She managed to turn away from him a little, but the wrist restraints limited her. She struggled to take comfort from the fact that she still wore her blouse and bra but had no doubt he could change that whenever he wanted — and he would want.

"It's about control, Shana," he said. "My control over you and your sexual nature, ultimate control over your actions and reactions."

He placed his free hand against her buttocks. Instead of using his grip to hold her in place, he swept that hand into her crack, all too easily finding and sealing her butt hole. At the same time, he worked his other hand into her pussy. Unable to distinguish between the two sensations, she looked down and back, panting in — in what? — anticipation?

The ankle cuffs left her with a reassuring amount of freedom, but if she did anything except try to clamp her legs together, he'd think she wanted this. And she didn't, did she?

Pressure built in her ass. Too late she realized he'd worked a finger into her back there. It felt as if he was determined to get his respective invading fingers to touch, pushing relentlessly while she stood there and accepted like some dumb animal.

Furious, she tried to wrench free. The strain in her arms reminded her of how securely she was being held in place, but she couldn't just give up control of her most intimate parts. Cursing into the disgusting ball, she turned her hips one way and then the other until somehow she managed to dislodge the finger up her cunt. She again tried to kick him but could only lift her leg a few inches. The hated invasion prodded at her butt, degrading and overwhelming at the same time.

"Fight is good, Shana." He spoke with his mouth close to her ear. "It tells me how far you have to go."

Go where?

Suddenly her ass felt empty, abandoned. She turned toward him, but he was gone. She spotted him back by the pulley. When he tightened the chain, she stood on tiptoes. If he pulled any more, she'd wind up suspended. Instead, he left her trying to balance her weight on her toes. Squatting, he took hold of her ankles and spread her legs wide. The strain in her arms became intense.

"It won't be like this long," he said. "As soon as I've done something, I'll..."

She wasn't sure, but she thought he'd removed the chain between the ankle cuffs. Before she could make sense of it, she felt something else being hooked to one of the cuffs. Unable to see what it was, she had no choice to wait. To her great relief, he let her down so she once more stood flat-footed.

He knelt behind her and forced her legs even further apart. Maybe she should have fought, but why try? He'd only pull her onto her toes again. After doing something with the other ankle, he patted her ass and stood up.

She tried to shift position but couldn't. Leaning forward, she saw he'd secured a metal bar not quite three feet long to the ankle cuffs, making it impossible for her to close her legs. Her wide stance left her pussy vulnerable. Accessible.

On the brink of screaming, a quick, hot emotion silenced her. She was helpless, his. But he'd promised he wouldn't hurt her.

Still, he could, and would, do whatever he wanted with her.

Heat snaked over her, starting with the top of her head and traveling throughout her until her entire body felt on fire. The flames between her legs leaped higher and higher until her pussy blazed. She was flooding herself, her arousal clear for him to see and understand.

No, not sexual heat, surely not! Fear, of course fear. And anger – a ton of anger.

"I've seen some of your magazine ads," he informed her. "Studied the way you carry yourself. I'm impressed by your athleticism and know it takes a lot of work to stay in shape. The camera loves you – that's what they say, isn't it? What do you think the camera would show now? Would it find the truth about yourself you're just discovering?"

Helpless. Her body belonged to him.

Chapter Four

Ranger stepped back and studied his captive. He knew his job and could do it in his sleep. Still, he delayed taking the next step. Maybe he should tell her he wasn't going to do this after all. She'd never know how close he'd come to the end of self-restraint and have no inkling of the beast beneath the clothes, but if he did, he'd have failed her and Recovery. Most of all, he might never know the truth about himself.

And that was vital.

She had to be wondering why he hadn't stripped off her blouse and bra, but he had his reasons for delaying taking that step. Soon enough she'd be naked, a sexual object instead of the competent businesswoman he'd met yesterday.

Her hot gaze told him she'd never again be quite the person she'd always been. Oh yes, when he allowed it, she'd put on clothes and close her legs, but right now she was offered up to a man, and she knew it.

What she didn't know was what beat inside the man.

And despite what he'd just told her, he didn't comprehend enough about her, yet.

Weary of the unrelenting debate, he walked over to the bed, picked up the large white vibrator with the knobbed tip and plugged it in, making sure she noted his every move. He figured she knew enough about sex tools to realize this one had more kick than something controlled by batteries.

Let her think about it.

She'd feel it soon enough, taste it, dance to its tune, but first... Positioning himself in front of her, he pressed his free hand against her pussy. After pushing firmly for several seconds, he started lightly slapping her labia. She groaned and struggled to get away but could manage only to roll her hips from side to side. He stopped and let her think about things for a little while, then took up slapping her external sex organs again. Each blow was slightly sharper than the previous one. He let the rhythm take over and become a drumbeat of flesh against flesh.

She now breathed in short gasps, and her pussy was so wet his palm kept slipping off her. When her gasps became a pant, he studied what he'd done. Her pussy had become red and swollen. With blood pooled there, she'd be even more responsive to what came next.

Careful not to let her see what he had in mind, he positioned the vibrator between her legs and pressed the textured tip against her clit. He turned it on again, going immediately to the highest speed.

She sobbed and tried to jump away. Despite her struggles, he easily kept the vibrator head on her clit, and although he was tempted to run it over her entire pussy so he could study her reaction, he concentrated on anticipating her movements. Her hips continued their unproductive twisting, and she kept trying to stand on tiptoe—as if that would do any good.

"Instinct is getting the better part of you," he observed. "Earlier I was going to commend you for your self-control, but rational thought and action only go so far. You want this and hate it at the same time. I hold the trigger." He briefly increased the pressure on the vibrator to make his point. "You can't control your reactions."

Although the sound was muffled, he had no doubt she'd just cursed him. After settling back on her heels, she tried turning from side to side. He easily matched her movements, enjoying the task of keeping her clit stimulated. If the tables were turned, and she was the one teasing his sex, he'd go off like the proverbial Roman firecracker, but they weren't. He was the puppet-master. Her pussy danced to his tune.

She shuddered, twisted, fought her bonds, tried to clamp her legs together, sweated and cursed.

Suddenly she stopped fighting. He might have thought her defeated if not for the strangled gasps telegraphing her impending climax. Knowing she'd hate him and knowing her hatred was better for both of them right now, he removed the vibrator from her. Screaming into the gag, she strained to glare at him.

"Not yet, Shana. Not until you've earned a climax and begged me to allow you to come." He lightly touched the still-vibrating toy to her swollen clit and watched her strong thigh muscles clench. Before she could leap over the edge, he pushed the off button but kept the vibrator against her. "Think about the promise in this tool of mine and ask yourself what you'll do to get me to use it on you again, this time long enough to let you come."

Although he knew better, he flicked his finger over her heat-ignited clit. It took so little to imagine his cock rubbing her there, satisfying both of them. Then struggling against himself, he got to his feet and removed her gag. He remained behind her, wondering what she'd do if he kissed her or gently ran his fingers through her hair or told her of lonely dreams.

But tenderness and openness wasn't part of the process. For him it had never been.

"You bastard!" she shouted. "You damnable bastard!"

"I'm sure," he agreed. "You probably figured this out but slapping your pussy gets the blood flowing. I can do that to you whenever I want. As for when or if I'll take you any further…"

"It isn't fair." She sounded less angry but still shaken. "What did I ever do to deserve—?"

"Deserve has nothing to do with it. Your journey into the cave has begun."

"What are we doing here?" she demanded. "You said this place belongs to Scarlet Cavern. How come you have access?"

"It doesn't matter. Let's just say this is part of the service you paid for."

* * * * *

What is the cave like, Shana wanted to ask, but she was once again alone in a dark room. He'd removed the bar between her legs and replaced it with the ankle restraints but hadn't re-chained her to the floor. He'd loosened the chain holding her hands over her head, giving her enough freedom that she could have masturbated if she felt like it. Damn it, she felt like it all right. She'd never come to the brink of a climax so fast in her life without so much as a hint of conventional foreplay, and although she knew it was a combination of feeling helpless and being slapped, the knowledge didn't help. Sweat caked her skin and cunt juice clung to her inner thighs. Her breasts felt too big for her bra. She also had to go to the bathroom.

When the pressure on her bladder became too much

to ignore, she tried crossing her legs and conjured up her memory of what the room looked like. There hadn't been a toilet. Did he intend her to wet and soil herself, increasing her degradation?

"Ranger, Ranger, damn it! Don't leave me like this."

When he didn't respond, she yelled again. She imagined he was just outside the door, enjoying her discomfort. Teeth clenched, she changed position but kept her legs clamped together.

"Ranger, I have to go to the bathroom."

Light flooded the room, and she briefly closed her eyes. He stood in the open doorway, looming like some ancient warrior between her and freedom. "Do you?" he said.

"Yes. Where—?"

"Say please."

"What?"

"If you want something, from now on you'll have to say please."

Fuck you. Much as she relished putting the shoe on the other foot, there was no denying he held the upper hand. "Please," she managed.

"Please, master."

She recoiled from the very idea of ever using the word, but until she'd done something about her full bladder, she was hardly in a position to negotiate.

"Please, master."

"Lacks conviction, but we'll get there. Oh, we will."

His warning distracted her from her discomfort. He walked toward her, freed her wrists, and dragged her behind him. He opened a door she hadn't noticed before, and she found herself looking at a large bathroom complete with large shower and a tub large enough for two.

Two.

Her swollen bladder snagged her attention. She started toward the toilet, but Ranger yanked her arms behind her and pushed up, forcing her to lean over. "You have so much to learn, so many changes to undergo." His tone was as rough as his control. "I own your body. And your mind will become part of my mastery."

You bastard!

"I'll let you pee this time because I need your focus to be on the lessons—and because I'm a compassionate master."

Bastard. But much as she loathed him, she couldn't argue with the fact that her strength was nothing compared to his. Slow and deliberate, he allowed her to straighten but didn't release his hold on her wrists. She stood with her back to him, her bladder aching and her mind locked on him. Feeling too much like a dumb animal being led to slaughter, she let him position her over the toilet. Only once she was seated did he release her. Not looking at him, she urinated. When she finished, she looked around for toilet paper.

"If I let you wipe yourself, what will you do to show your gratitude?"

He'd anticipated her furious glare, but that didn't stop him from hating to see her loathing. "Gratitude?" she spat. "How can you—? Wait, it's part of the control thing, isn't it?"

"Yes."

She nodded, her features sober. "And Lindsay went

through the same degradation?"

"Yes."

"Oh God." Her eyes filmed. "What-what do I have to do?"

The first small and uncertain step had been taken. He wondered if she knew she'd crossed over a line from which there was no return. "Take off your blouse."

She did so without expression, the movement quick and efficient then gave it to him. He took it and dropped it on the counter. Her full breasts pressed against the pale pink bra, her nipples hard and swollen. After studying them openly for the better part of a minute, he reached into the cupboard and handed her a new roll. She dropped her gaze as she removed the packaging and wiped herself. She slowly stood, glancing at him repeatedly as if assuring herself he'd approve. "I-I'd like to wash my hands," she said.

"I imagine you would."

"May I?"

"Not yet."

Clasping her hands together in front of her pussy, she stood waiting. He didn't want to hurt for her or care what was happening to her sense of self, but he did. She reminded him of a yearling filly with a bit in her mouth for the first time.

"The bra."

She recoiled but nodded as if expecting the order. Although he would have loved to handle this chore, he simply watched as she reached behind her and unfastened the hooks. This final piece of disrobing had to be her act. Otherwise, she could always tell herself she'd resisted.

After pulling the bra off her breasts and shoulders, she handed the garment to him, but he refused to take it. After a moment, she let it fall to the floor.

"Wash. Quickly," he said. "Back to the room," he ordered when she was done because looking at her generous breasts had suddenly made the bathroom too small for him. He'd broken a number of horses during the two summers he'd spent on a ranch owned by a friend of his father. The two men had decided that hard physical work would toughen the boy up for following in his old man's footsteps, and in many respects they'd been right. Working with horses had taught him the essential difference between destroying an animal's spirit and leaving it with a sense of self while cementing the lesson of who was in charge.

The same skills had served him well when he'd been deemed ready to enter Scarlet Cavern's world. Over time, he'd learned to separate his emotions from the task at hand, but Shana wasn't a wild horse or eager-to-comply submissive woman. Proud and independent, she'd come to him because she wanted to save her best friend. He didn't know how to handle her courage and commitment — or his reactions.

What reaction? What emotions? Their time together was about lessons taught and learned. He knew how to do that — maybe it was all he knew.

And maybe the years and nights alone had stripped away his defenses.

She'd walked obediently ahead of him back into the room without tripping on her ankle restraints and now stood with her arms at her sides, fingers clenched. How long had it been since he'd been alone like this with a woman, her wanting more than to be fucked, him needing more than a place to house his cum?

"Turn around," he said. Could she tell how shaken he felt?

"What are you going to do?"

"Turn around!"

Her eyes became big and dark. He noted a faint trembling in her legs and struggled to think about that instead of what it would feel like to have her embrace him, to want to spend the night with him — and longer. When she'd positioned herself as he'd commanded, he left her and walked over to the dresser. She looked over her shoulder at him, her attention on the soft cotton rope and smaller ball gag he'd chosen. He paused, waiting to see if she'd say things had gone far enough. When she didn't, he looped the rope over his shoulder, then slipped the gag into place. He allowed her to examine the ball with her fingers before he ordered her to cross her wrists behind her. Although her nostrils flared and her whole body shook, she did as he ordered.

A wave of admiration swept over him. He fought it by concentrating on running loop after loop of the silky rope just above her elbows so her arms were pulled back, her breasts thrusting out. Then he secured her wrists, leaving enough length for the rest of what he intended to do. But first...

Loving the feel of her straining muscles, he stroked her upper arms. Her breathing had no rhythm and drool had already formed around the ball. He wiped it away then dried his fingers by wiping them on her breasts.

"Ownership," he said. "My ownership of you." *For now.*

Eyes all but bulging, she shook her head so vigorously

that her glossy blonde hair flew about. The movement reminded him of fillies trying to rid themselves of bridles they wore for the first time. The horses had never won the battle, neither would Shana.

His swollen cock pressed painfully against his jeans in anticipation of what he planned to do next. But although he'd give anything to strip off every shred of clothing and join her in sex, his staying dressed served as an undeniable message about the differences between their statuses. Breaking this strong and independent woman would be as much work as breaking a wild horse, but he knew how to do his job. *His job, nothing more.*

Hoping he could judge his arousal well enough to know when he'd pushed himself as far as he dared, he cupped his hands over her breasts. He handled them, not to tease and tantalize, but as a cowboy might examine a piece of horseflesh he was contemplating buying. As he stroked, pressed, pinched, and lifted, he studied her reaction. Her eyes said she hated his cavalier handling of what belonged to her but hadn't yet been pushed to her personal wall. When he grabbed her nipples and started rubbing them between thumbs and forefingers, she back-stepped. What she muttered behind the gag was no lover's hot whisper.

He kept after her, pinching just hard enough to flirt with pain. He matched her step for step until he'd backed her against the bed. When she tried to twist free, he pushed her onto the bed. Her roped arms were trapped under her, forcing her to arch in a way that turned her breasts into an offering. Smiling deliberately, he pulled her breasts away from her body, stretching them. Cursing a garbled curse, she struggled to roll away. He stopped her by climbing onto the bed and straddling her. He released her breasts but settled his weight on her pelvis.

"Trying to fight free is natural," he told her. "It's the body's self-preservation instinct. Only a few people can override it."

He let her absorb that a moment. Then he wiped away the drool that had reformed, this time drying his fingers in her hair. His cock screamed.

"Wanting to own your body means you're alive," he continued. "What I want to show you is that it's possible to override that impulse by keying into another basic instinct—the one for sex. Ready?"

She nodded. Under him, her muscles turned to steel. How he'd love to see her working out! She didn't try to push him off. Rather her response, he knew, came from her comprehension of what he'd just told her. "If you're fully into what's happening, you're going to come to hate your body. Hate your sexuality. At the same time, your clit will become the source of your greatest pleasure—but you'll experience that pleasure only at my hands. You'll hate me. Hell, you already hate me. But you'll come to the point when your need, not just for answers about your friend, but for what I can give you overrides your loathing of both of us."

Her muscles continued to feel like coiled springs, prompting him to demonstrate his mastery in a way that tested his own self-control. Making sure she knew what he intended, he leaned over her and began licking her breasts. He stroked her over and over again, keeping his tongue wet so she'd feel his moist heat. Bit by bit she relaxed. Her curses faded to be replaced by moans.

He kept at her, losing himself in what was no longer a lesson, no longer punishment. He loved her with his mouth, his tongue and learned her taste, texture, essence. His teeth lightly kissed her, and he lost the distinction between their flesh. She rocked from side to side. Her back arched even more, and her skin became as hot as his mouth and cock.

He'd free her. In his mind, he removed the bonds and turned his body over to her. He'd lost the distinction between them and whisper of things he'd never told another person. She'd accept his honesty, his gifts, and understand his need to put isolation behind him. In this place where time had no meaning, they'd reveal their pasts to each other and share dreams of the future. Most of all, he'd trust her with his soul.

When he couldn't take any more of his useless dreams, he left, carrying the spreader bar with him.

* * * * *

Shana's breasts had dried and flesh that had recently felt hot to the point of flames was now cold. Under her, her arms and shoulders ached, but she couldn't put her mind to changing position. Breathing was far from easy, and she hated slobbering. She couldn't say whether she hated Ranger or herself more. *Damn you, Lindsay. Look what you've made me do!*

Men had sucked on her breasts before, not many if truth be known, but enough for her to determine she didn't particularly enjoy what they obviously considered foreplay. The trouble was, those men had been so self-focused they hadn't tried to put themselves in her position. Did they really think a woman liked her breasts treated as if she was a nursing cat?

It had been different with Ranger—God, had it! It was, hell it was almost as if he'd crawled into her skin and knew what she craved. She couldn't bring herself to admit she liked being at his mercy — was that what it was? — but there was no denying she'd been turned on.

She still was.

She was also damn uncomfortable she admitted as she rolled onto her side and sat up. As he'd done before, he'd left without giving her a hint of when he'd return. She hoped it would be soon because otherwise she'd lose feeling in her arms. It wasn't that the ropes were all that uncomfortable, but she'd never had her elbows pulled together like this — in a tie that felt ridiculously erotic.

Erotic?

Well, she chided herself, what else would you call it?

She was still sitting on the side of the bed waiting for what she wasn't sure when he walked back in. Of course she couldn't ask where he'd gone or what he intended to do now he'd returned which only added to the anticipation licking at her nerve endings. She didn't remember ever being this aware of her body before, as if her whole being had narrowed down to being a woman in the most carnal of ways.

God but he was beautiful! Zoos repulsed her because she hated the contrast between nature's creatures and cold bars, but this man — this owner of her body — exuded everything she considered wild.

"Have you had some time to think?" he asked. His tone was casual as if he was asking her what she thought of the weather. "I'm sorry if I interrupted you, but you'll have plenty of time to consider the changes you're undertaking — and anticipate what other changes I have in mind."

He walked toward her, his steps slow and measured,

and his attention remained on her eyes as if seeking to learn her secrets while keeping his own. Before she could gather the courage to ask what he was keeping locked inside, he took hold of her nipples. She sucked in her breath but otherwise did nothing to try to distance herself from him. He was right, anticipation had turned her half-wild with wondering what came next.

Although she intended to study his expression so maybe she'd be ready for him, his manipulation of her breasts distracted her. She'd been proud of them and hadn't been looking forward to what gravity would eventually do to them. Unless she'd read him wrong, Ranger flat out enjoyed rolling her nipples between thumb and forefinger. The sensual manipulation might turn painful, but she'd enjoy his touch for what it was—a man's appreciation of a woman's natural C-cups.

Only it was more than appreciation. As he ran his nails over her areolas, she was forced to acknowledge that for as long as he desired, her breasts belonged to him.

And not just her breasts.

Without warning, he pushed her back on the bed. "On your side," he ordered.

Not comprehending, she stared at him. Grabbing her around the waist, he forced her onto a hip and slapped her buttocks hard. "On your side," he repeated.

Although she was already halfway into the position, she struggled to manipulate her upper body as he'd ordered. She was turned away from him now and facing the wall. She tried to look back, but he yanked her feet up toward her buttocks. She forced herself to submit while he removed the metal restraints and lashed lengths of rope over her ankles. Next he tied more rope to her bound wrists and secured hands and feet so she was securely hogtied. He rolled her toward him, bringing her breasts and pelvis within easy reach again.

"How does that feel?" he asked with his hands posed inches from her helpless flesh. "Not exactly the modern independent woman anymore, are you?"

His tone had turned husky which made her even more nervous. He started stroking her thighs. At the same time, he pressed a hand over her belly and held her in place. His hands were somewhat rough and created a mind-snagging friction on flesh that seldom saw the light of day. He kept his touch featherlight, the tickling sensation centering in her cunt. For a long time, he confined his gliding caresses to the outside of both thighs until she thought she might scream for wanting more. Then bit by impossible bit, his fingers slid closer to the apex of her legs. The hand on her belly started massaging her, making it all but impossible to decide which manipulation to concentrate on. She felt strain in her shoulders and taut thigh muscles, the semi-discomfort polar opposites from his hot and wonderful fingers.

She began to melt under him, flesh and bone heating.

Although her eyes refused to focus, she knew he was coming closer. When she realized he intended to take her breast into his mouth again, she arched toward him. Of their own will, her knees parted. He closed his mouth over an aching mound, sucking and tonguing her nipple at the same time. She moaned into the ball and fought to remain still. She twitched when his hand slipped between her legs.

Although she managed to swallow another moan, there was no hiding the reality of her flooding pussy. This man owned her, claimed her. She belonged to him, needed to belong, wanted nothing else in life.

Still suckling, he ran a finger into her and pressed. Her legs opened as much as the bonds allowed as she offered her sex to him, offered him everything. He released her breast and settled himself on the edge of the bed. His weight caused her to slide against his hip, but he kept his finger inside her.

When she settled, he began playing with her pussy lips, her clit. Every touch of nail or knuckle resulted in another strangled-sounding moan. She couldn't stop her head from thrashing.

A climax! So close.

"Responsive," he whispered in the strangled tone that drove her half-mad. "Your sex rules you, Shana."

It never has before.

"It's your greatest weakness." As if proving his point, he slipped his middle finger up her so she now had two fingers inside her. She felt filled by him, no longer separate. "A highly sexed woman is vulnerable. She can never turn off her sexuality and the right man can always control her."

I don't want...

Before she could finish the thought, he pulled out of her and wiped her cunt juice on her belly. He pushed her legs together, squeezing a bit harder than necessary. Between her clamped thighs, her sex organs wept.

"You want more of what I was giving you, don't you?" The question was rhetorical. "Right now you'd cut off your right arm for a climax, wouldn't you?"

She hated him! Wanted him and his knowledge of her body out of her life!

"Not going to answer, are you? I understand, Shana. You're afraid of what's happening to you and your lack of control." Releasing her legs, he slipped his hand under her buttocks and rolled her onto her belly. "I know which buttons to push, when and where, how much. You can hardly wait to see what I'm going to do next."

After patting her butt, he stood up. She heard him walk back to the dresser where he'd gotten the ropes. Waiting for him, not moving because he'd only put her back where he wanted her, she struggled to think of anything other than the fire he'd created in her. He was right, damn him. She loved sex. Her body craved release on a regular basis, and she'd become an expert in giving it what it needed when necessary.

Knowing he possessed the same skills and more terrified her.

He sat beside her again and parted her ass cheeks. She shuddered at the thought of him studying her butt and what his plans for it were. Then he slipped something hard and cold inside her ass, and she sobbed into the bed.

"A butt plug, Shana."

The foreign object filled her. He'd inserted it so deeply she wondered what it would take to extricate it. If she had use of her hands, she reassured herself, she'd have no trouble yanking it out and throwing it as far as she could. But she was helpless.

Helpless and excited.

After repositioning the bulky and already heated intrusion, he rolled her onto her back again. Once more he left her, this time to turn off the light. She strained to hear him, then tried to slide away when he grabbed her by the ankles.

"Not going to happen." He punctuated the obvious by pressing on her hips. "You're mine, remember. No matter how long the lesson takes, we'll keep at it until you willingly give ownership of your body over to me."

Willingly? Never!

Don't lie, Shana. You came into this with your eyes wide open. He told you what to expect, asked permission. And you gave it.

He started untying the rope that held her wrists and ankles together. "Your contract with Recovery is of a limited duration. When you're reunited with your friend and give her the option of saying at Scarlet Cavern or leaving, you'll never have anything to do with me again."

He helped her straighten her legs, and as she reveled in the regained circulation, he began freeing her ankles. "But you'll never forget what took place between us. I don't think you want to."

She didn't resist when he spread her legs wide apart. Locked in darkness, she couldn't focus on anything except his hands roaming over her calves, knees, and thighs, didn't try to force herself to remain still as his hands approached her pussy. Lying on her bound hands wasn't particularly comfortable, and she couldn't say she liked the feel of the butt plug.

Before she could begin to prepare, he ran a finger over her hot, hard clit. Tasting a climax, she tried to close her legs and trap him against her. Just like that, he left her sex wanting and forced her legs apart. When he released them, she tried to assume a more comfortable position.

"No!" He punctuated the command by slapping one breast and then the other. "You do what I tell you, nothing else. Now, sit up."

She struggled to obey but lacked the necessary leverage. He hauled her toward him, and she balanced her weight on her butt and the plug while he untied her hands. Having learned her lesson, she kept them behind her.

"Progress," he acknowledged and drew her hands in front of her. Pinpricks of sensation in her shoulders pulled her focus there and made her slow to realize he was retying her hands in front. Then he pushed her back down and ran his hands over the inside of her thighs in a silent order for her to keep herself spread.

When he pulled her hands over her head, she focused on that. Something clicked in place. She gave an experimental tug and found he'd secured her hands to something at the head of the bed.

Was there no limit to the things he could do to her?

Chapter Five

Shana knew not to resist when Ranger roped her ankles and tied them to the sides of the bed, splaying her legs. With her cunt so exposed, she supposed she should be grateful for the darkness, but she'd rather watch her captor.

Only he wasn't her captor because she'd asked for this.

Pondering her insanity made her slow to realize he wasn't content with simply securing her ankles. He also wrapped more of the soft rope around her thighs and tied them in the same way he had her ankles. Next he did the same to her knees. She could still move her upper body a little, but from the waist down, she was helpless, his.

"The lessons aren't easy."

I know that! You don't need...

He spread a hand over her breast and grasped it tightly. Not breathing, she waited for either a caress or squeeze. Instead, he held it as surely as he'd tied her legs. A moment later, she felt warm metal clamp around her nipple. The sharp pinch caused her to try to sit up, but of course she couldn't. Panting, she waited for the next assault. It came in the form of another clip on her other nipple. When the discomfort subsided, she became aware of a slight weight between her breasts and realized a thin chain stretched from one clamp to the other.

Ranger gripped the chain and lifted it, putting strain

on her breasts. "Bondage knows no limits. That's part of Scarlet Cavern's creeds — an exploration of the vast world of loss of freedom and its effects on both slaves and masters."

Slaves? Masters? No! But even as her mind struggled against the words, she couldn't deny the truth. Tonight Ranger owned her body.

She'd surrendered it to him.

His manipulation of her breasts didn't hurt that much. In truth, the sensation added to the sexual electricity humming through her. She continued to drip and could smell herself. So could he, she reluctantly admitted. Playing the submissive had never been her *thing*, at least she'd never known a man she felt like exploring bondage with, but sometimes at night, with her own fingers inside her, she fantasized about being rendered helpless while a man claimed her in every way.

Well, she acknowledged as Ranger released the chain and began caressing her belly, fantasy had become reality.

His fingers felt like electric pinpricks. He touched her hips, thighs, waist, breasts, her sides. He stroked her armpits, not to tickle but in an undeniable message that even this part of her belonged to him. When he covered her throat and gave it a firm squeeze, she got the message. Her life was in his hands.

When she thought she'd lose her mind with wanting her vagina touched, he changed position. From the pressure on the mattress, she guessed he was kneeling near the foot of the bed.

Something feathery slid over her already swollen labia. She no longer felt the strain in her legs, dismissed her bound hands, even the gag and nipple clips. He stroked her with whatever he was using, and she struggled to lift her hips off the bed to give him greater access. Over and over again he treated her to the silken strands. She existed only between her legs, danced at the edge of a climax, and reveled in her own sexuality. His touches said he considered her cunt her most prized possession, and he knew how to give the ultimate pleasure. Then he replaced the toy with his fingers, still stroking, still burrowing her deep in sensation and she would have done anything for him. Become anything.

"Pleasure," he whispered, his tone husky. "Pleasure comes in many forms. The goal of Scarlet Cavern is to experiment with all those forms, even those the submissive initially fights."

His voice held a warning note, but she couldn't concentrate on anything beyond her throbbing clit and hot, swollen folds. Her core felt flooded and ready for his cock. He *had* to know what she was offering; he *had* to.

"Pleathe," she sobbed into the gag. "Fuck me."

"Damn you. Damn you."

"Pleathe!"

"No!"

He gave her no warning, allowed her no opportunity to prepare. When he turned the caressing toy into a whip and smacked her sensitive crotch, she sobbed and fought her bonds.

"Not going to help." He stuck her again. "Fight all you want. Wear yourself out." Another smack. "It won't change anything."

Blow after blow rained down on her. Whatever he was using was too soft to cause damage, and she couldn't call the beating painful. But the invasion — the unrelenting and intimate assault on her sex…

He was never going to stop! He'd keep at her until he'd stripped every ounce of responsiveness out of her, until she hated him! No matter that she couldn't so much as turn to the side, she kept trying to escape him and what was both humiliation and ecstasy. She yanked on the wrist restraints, tried to bite the ball forcing her mouth open, struggled against the trio of ropes on each leg.

And as she did, he kept striking her. She could no longer separate her clit from the rest of her sexual organs, lost the distinction between inner passage and outer lips. She'd been reduced to a mare in heat, a bitch dog, a piece of flesh, had become a cunt.

Pleasure! *No, it can't be!* But as her pussy continued to heat, there was no denying the truth. He knew everything about her, owned everything. Being assaulted like this felt incredible! And she loathed him for her response.

"Hate me do you?" he taunted. "Not because you're afraid I'll hurt you, but because I know things about your body you didn't. Can make it do things you didn't know it was capable of. At the same time, I'm a stranger, some man you hired, a voice in the dark. Nothing more."

He moved closer and started trailing the whip over her mons. "Make-believe is one thing. There probably isn't a woman alive who doesn't fantasize about being hauled off by a savage and turned into his sex slave." The whip caressed her belly, waist, breasts. "But you never expected it to turn into the real thing. Reality is different, isn't it?"

Something slipped inside her. For a wild moment she believed it was his cock. Then she realized the invasion was too hard. Frightened, she strained to see, but the night kept its secrets.

"Not a dildo," he informed her. He spun the object in a slow circle. "Feel the heat. It's warm because I was holding it in my hand." He reversed direction. "It's the crop's handle."

"Nahhhh!"

"Freshly washed." The handle pushed in further, then retreated a little, pushed again. "Not exactly the same sensation as you get from a cock," he said as he increased its speed and depth. "But close enough. Feel it. Feel everything. What do you think? Can I make you come with a leather handle?"

No! You're disgusting!

The gag kept her from lying, but as her mind again sank into her pussy, she imagined Ranger between her legs, his cock buried in her, pleasuring both of them. She'd cling to him as waves of pleasure racked her body. His thrusts would become harder, stronger. Their flesh would all but melt together, and they'd scream out their climaxes at the same time.

And in the aftermath of fucking, she'd kiss this stranger and whisper...

She didn't realize she'd been gasping for air until Ranger abruptly removed the gag. Her tongue still felt pinched, and her lips ached. The handle remained in her, inert now.

"Talk to me, Shana," he muttered. She could tell his mouth was only inches from her ears. "Tell me what you want me to do."

"No! No, I'm not—"

"Yes, you are." He punctuated his comment by wiping her drool off her with the bedspread. "Your pussy can't lie."

"I hate you!"

He took a deep breath and briefly ran his knuckles lightly over her jaw. "I expect you do." His tone sounded regret-laden. "But if you're being honest with yourself, you now know you need me, not just so you can get to your friend, but because you're a woman and I'm a man. A man experienced in commanding a female's sexuality."

She needed to concentrate on what he was telling her and the emotion behind his words, but her wet cavern still housed what he'd put in her. "I want up! Let me go."

"For real?"

"No. No," she whispered.

"I didn't think so. What happened just then? You couldn't bring yourself to admit I'm right?"

She'd die before she'd admit anything to him. Right now, silence was her best weapon. Hell, if truth be told, words—or lack thereof—were the only weapons she had. Any sense of accomplishment she might have gained from clamping her teeth together evaporated when he turned his attention back to the whip handle. It moved effortlessly in her saturated passage, sliding back and forth and up and down at the same time.

Her traitorous body bucked toward him. Although the strain in her legs was becoming uncomfortable, it held only a small part of her attention. Under his expert guidance, again and again she surged to the brink of a climax only to be yanked back at the last instant.

"Don't, don't, don't," she managed.

"Don't what?"

"I can't—I can't take this. Ranger, please!"

When he pulled the handle out of her, she insanely

prayed he'd replace it with his cock. Instead, he pressed against her pulsing bud. Her pussy muscles clenched. She gasped and stared at the edge of the abyss.

"Wouldn't take much, would it?" he asked with her clit caught between his thumb and forefinger. "The right trigger and you'd be there."

"Yes!"

"But if I let you come, you wouldn't want or need me anymore — at least for awhile."

She sobbed and tried to push her sex at him. To her horror, he released her. Her cry ended with a curse.

"Do you want me to beg?" she demanded. "Is that what you want, for me to grovel?"

Instead of answering, he set about untying her legs. Once they were free, he pushed them together in a silent but undeniable message that he was done with her.

"How can you be so-so cruel?"

"So you'll understand my power. A power that echoes what goes on at Scarlet Cavern."

* * * * *

After releasing Shana's hands, Ranger grabbed the breast chain and used it to lead her out of the training room and into the kitchen. A dull thunk let him know the butt plug had slipped out. No matter. He'd reinsert it when he was ready or rather when he had to.

He sat on a stool at the counter and ordered her to fix them dinner. Instead, she stood naked in the middle of the modern kitchen, hands fisted and shaking. He felt the same way, his head throbbing from the effort of keeping her at arms' length. He'd gone too far back in there. Damn it, didn't he know his own limits where this woman was concerned? The outside world saw a well-honed body designed to show off expensive athletic wear, but he'd found the primitive animal under the exterior layers—a woman capable of matching the primitive man he was.

If their bodies were as one, what about their minds, their hearts?

"Wha-what do you want to eat?" she asked in a broken whimper.

"The refrigerator is well-stocked," he said, grateful for the distraction. "You probably won't want to fry anything. I'd hate to see you burn yourself."

"With-with this still on?" She indicated the nipple clips.

"Do they hurt?"

He could tell she was debating the answer and prepared to hear a lie. Instead, she sighed. "No."

"Good, because I like seeing them." *I love looking at everything about you.*

She turned her back on him and opened the refrigerator door. As she went about preparing a fruit salad and ham and cheese sandwiches, he studied her every movement. He'd deliberately positioned himself behind the counter so she couldn't see his erection. Shit, he'd give anything to unzip himself and order her to take his cock in her mouth, but he didn't dare.

This wasn't easy. Hell, this was hard! Shana's model's body was fantastic! She obviously treated it with respect and from the looks of her muscled arms and legs, she worked out regularly. Even if she hadn't, her breasts would have challenged him. And he didn't dare think about what waited between her legs.

And yet more than her body turned him on. She was

one highly sexed woman. He'd have to be dead not to have deduced that from the time she'd spent under his control. Back when the dark side had ruled him, he'd handled every imaginable kind of woman. Whether rebellious or meek, they all eventually surrendered their separate selves to him, but those women had come to Scarlet Cavern because they craved something they weren't getting from their ordinary lives.

Shana wasn't driven by selfishness. Instead, she'd decided to risk it all for the woman she considered her best friend. He couldn't imagine caring that much about another human being—and wished he could. For the first time in his life he craved knowledge about more than a woman's body.

She served him at the counter and stared at her plate. "Do you want—can I eat?"

"You're learning. Yes, you may eat. Then it'll be time for another lesson."

Her eyes widened, and she took what he decided was an involuntary backward step. "No," she whispered.

"We don't have much time."

She dragged her fingers through her hair then glanced down at her breasts as if belatedly realizing what the gesture was doing to them. "I can't...I can't take any more right now."

"Yes, you can." He took a large bite of sandwich and took his time chewing. She looked on the verge of bolting. The thought of running her down stirred his senses, but he merely watched her. She'd been staring at the floor but now lifted her head.

"Do you like this?" she asked. "Beating me down, making me half-crazy from wanting sex, does it turn you on?"

He didn't need to answer. Hell, he owed her nothing of himself. But he was teaching her to look at herself in the most primitive way and although he understood the danger, he suddenly wanted to do the same. "Yeah, it turns me on. You're a beautiful woman, strong and vulnerable, committed in a way I don't understand."

She extended her hand, and for a heartbeat, he thought she meant to touch him. *Do it, please. Make me feel part of you.* Instead, she picked up her sandwich. "You should have kept the gag in my mouth. That way we wouldn't have to communicate."

"Oh, we're communicating." He nodded at her crotch to prove his point and fought his lonely admission of a moment ago.

Her mouth sagged, and she seemed to draw into herself. "My body is being honest," she whispered. "I can't stop it."

"I know what buttons to push," He admitted.

"Yes, you do."

She didn't add *damn it*, but he thought he heard the unspoken words. "What does it feel like," he asked, "to have someone else in charge of your body?"

Now it was her turn to concentrate on her meal. Watching her chew, he thought of those soft lips on his hard cock. In his fantasy, he no longer worked for Recovery and she didn't have a friend in the Cavern. Instead, they'd become a man and a woman intent on endlessly exploring new aspects of sexuality And more. Elements of the heart he barely comprehended.

"I-I want to say I hate it," she finally admitted. "I should. Hell, there's no way I should want to be handled like a side of beef."

"You're hardly that."

She shrugged, and the gesture caused the nipple chain to dance over her flesh. She touched it gingerly. "Caught," she whispered. "Trapped by my sexuality." Fingers shaking, she picked up her sandwich again.

"You feel trapped by your pussy?"

He thought she'd cringe or curse him. Instead, she regarded him for a long time before speaking. "I like sex. Hell, I love it. But there's always been—oh, I don't know—a sense that something's missing."

But now, with me, you're beginning to comprehend what that something is. And the terrifying thing is, so am I.

"Missing. Tell me, what are your fantasies?"

Again she seemed to shrink inside herself. He was glad she hadn't asked the question because he'd have to tell her he didn't have any fantasies. Maybe the boy he'd been a million years ago had dreamed, but he knew that to stay sane, he didn't dare revisit his childhood. Still, he wanted to lay everything before her.

"I-I'm not going to tell you."

He lingered over another bite of the meal he couldn't taste. Except for the chain and nipple clamps and her naked state, they were equals, two bodies and minds finding each other. "If I wanted to, I could wring everything from you."

She shuddered and looked around.

"The doors are locked."

He thought she might bolt. Instead, he felt the effort of her pulling herself together. "What-what do I have to do?" she asked.

Give yourself to me. And want the same from me. "Nothing because I know what your fantasies are without your having to say a word." He ached with wanting to pull her onto his lap but didn't trust himself to touch her. "I might not have all the details worked out yet, but your body has told me a lot."

He waited for that to sink in, then continued. "In your dreams you're a princess, maybe the queen. Savages attack the kingdom, and the leader drags you off to his cave. He rips off your clothes and chains you to the wall and rapes you, only it isn't rape because you want it."

She dropped her sandwich on the plate and backed up until she ran into the counter behind her. Hands cupped over her pubic area, she stared at him.

"At first you fight. You know you're supposed to and you're not sure; maybe he intends to kill you. But bit by bit your former life slips away, and you become *his*. Whatever he wants, you do it because his needs have become yours."

Believing he'd gotten at the truth, at least her side of it, he concentrated on his meal. What he lacked the courage to confess was his need to experience the same thing.

* * * * *

He was too big, too knowing.

Although she didn't know how, Shana managed to force down most of her dinner. She spent too long cleaning up, but at length there was nothing left to do. Scared and excited, she stood in the middle of the kitchen. "What were you doing before you, ah, took me on as a client?"

"I'd just finished a job."

"What kind? I know you can't give me the specifics,

but surely you can tell me something. Was it like this?"

"No. I worked with the president of a Fortune 500 company. Someone on the inside was stealing from them. I infiltrated the business and found out who, how, and why. Because a public disclosure would have shaken the company's credibility with investors, everything was handled privately."

"And the company has recovered financially?"

"They're getting there. Turn around," he said.

We're back to lessons, back to control. Feeling disconnected from her body, she did as this man who acted as if he owned her ordered. She tried not to think about his gaze running over her back, waist, the swell of her buttocks, down her legs, but she couldn't stop herself. Working out and running had honed her body in ways that had kept her employed and made her attractive to men. Always before she'd taken pride and pleasure in the attention her well-honed body brought her way, but none of the men who'd whistled or stared had stripped off her clothes and fastened clamps over her nipples.

"Firm ass," he said. "Long, lean legs. Ugly feet."

Despite herself, she chuckled. "Not my best feature."

"Side view now."

Still disassociated from her body, she made a quarter turn. She didn't know what to do with her hands so wrapped them around her waist. She was acutely aware of her belly and the apex of her legs and wondered whether he liked a woman with pubic hair. Maybe she should have shaved more than a bikini line.

No!

"Front view. Arms at your sides."

She'd only been to a livestock auction once, but the memory of cattle and horses being led into the arena solidified in her mind. Wondering how she'd feel if a man bid on her, she did as he ordered.

"They'll love you at Scarlet Cavern."

"I'm not—"

"Hands between your legs. I want to see you stroke yourself."

A minute ago, she'd been stacking plates in the dishwasher. Now he wanted...

"Take hold of your lips. Pull on them. Separate them and put your finger inside yourself."

"I..."

Before she could decide how or if to finish the sentence, he strode around the counter and took hold of the chain. Using it as a leash, he led her back into the room he'd imprisoned her in. She wanted to resist but feared hurting her nipples. Besides, this was about Lindsay. For Lindsay. Suddenly he stopped. "Pick it up."

To her shock she realized he was referring to the butt plug. She stared at him.

He slapped a breast. "Pick it up!"

Afraid to defy him, she knelt and retrieved the item.

"On the bed," he ordered. "On your belly."

How did this happen? I don't want...

A sharp sting on her ass sent her scrambling onto the bed on her hands and knees. She still held the plug. *Lindsay, I don't know if I can...*

"Put it back in."

"What?"

"Did you hear me? Back in!" He punctuated his order with another slap to her buttocks.

She rolled onto her side and reached behind her. It took some maneuvering, but she finally managed to insert it. Tears burning and trembling, she waited.

"Flat on your belly. Arms out."

Oh please. Please! I need a break, time to pull myself together. Still, she obeyed. As soon as she'd complied, he shoved the butt plug in as deep as it would go. Then he pushed her ass cheeks together as if sealing it in place.

"Hands behind your back."

An image of Lindsay writhing under a whipping surfaced in her mind and hating both her body and Ranger's knowledge of it, she did as he ordered. This time the wrists restraints felt like leather. She waited for him to secure her elbows as he'd done before. Instead, he stroked her buttocks and the back of her thighs until her clitoris caught fire. He could be tender. Beneath the intense lessons lay a man with soul; bit by bit she was learning that. The growing knowledge sustained her.

When he ran rope over her legs just above her knees, she forced herself to remain still. Once he'd secured her legs together, he ran more loops below her knees, then rolled her over onto her back. The butt plug pressed against tender flesh, filling her and awakening her need.

His expression neutral, he bent her knees and left her like that while he got something from the drawer. He held the long, thick red dildo up so she could see it, then loosened the rope around her thighs, separated her knees as far as they would go and unceremoniously ran the dildo into her. Because she was wet from the previous stimulation, it went in easily. The dildo filled her, unmoving—for now.

After another trip to the drawer, he showed her a new length of soft white rope. As she lay there like a trussed chicken, he looped the rope around her body under her breasts, then over them in a crisscross manner. Much as she wanted to close her eyes and disassociate herself from what he was doing to her, she couldn't. Finally he looped the rope around her breasts so the constrained globes stuck out from her chest.

He leaned down and licked the sides of her breasts.

"Tell me you don't like it, Shana. Tell me you hate what I'm doing to you."

"I hate…"

He licked again, the gesture slow and warm and erotic. When he exhaled, she felt his damp breath on her breasts like a kiss. "Finish what you were saying, unless you don't want to lie."

Lie! Tell him you loathe…

Before she could force out the words, he reached between her legs and touched the dildo. A buzzing sensation spread throughout her pussy. Caught in sensation, she stared at the ceiling. He kicked up the vibration a notch.

"Don't like this either, do you?" he said in a husky tone that drove her half-crazy. "Sure enough, I can tell this is the last thing you want me to do."

Her thigh muscles went slack. She couldn't think beyond the hard, hot vibrations or the wild way her clit responded. Sobbing, she collapsed on her bound wrists. As she settled on the mattress, the butt plug ran deeper.

Disconcerted, she tried to shift position, but he turned her legs to the side and drew her feet close to her ass. On her hip and shoulder now, she could do nothing except wait for his next more. Anticipate. His expression was unreadable as he worked the dildo back and forth, back and forth.

The sensation should have been familiar. After all, she'd done the same to herself enough times, but she'd never tied herself up or tried combining insertions in both openings. The biggest difference, however, had everything to do with the strong and all-knowing man who'd laid claim to her.

"Dance to its tune," he challenged as the vibrations became even stronger. From belly to thighs she was in motion, everything melting together, on fire.

No, not a fire! Climax! Please!

"No, no, no." Ranger punctuated his command by abruptly withdrawing the dildo.

In the still aftermath, she tried to hit her head against the bed. "Please, please, please," she chanted. "I can't take — I can't take this!"

"You don't have a choice."

She tried to rock onto her back but he kept her on her side. When she stopped struggling, he placed the juice-soaked dildo between her thighs and positioned himself so she could see him. Surely his eyes hadn't been this dark before, the line of his mouth so hard. "I'm going to lose my mind," she admitted through numb lips.

"If you do, you'll be the first woman it has happened to."

How many other women have there been? "Why are you doing this?"

"You know."

"You broke my friend down? Is that how you got her to submit to-to the things I saw?"

"Not me."

She knew that, didn't she? Maybe not. Everything was so confusing. When he reached for her breasts, she held her breath. She couldn't say whether she wanted him to touch her — whether she'd survive. He unclipped the nipple clamps and massaged her tender nubs before draping the chain over her throat. Next he undid the elaborately tied ropes he'd placed over her breasts and dropped the lengths on her belly.

"Not you," she finally thought to say. "But someone has-has broken her down."

"She won't agree that's what happened."

Does that mean I'm going to see her? When? And what do I have to do to make it happen? "Ranger?" She swallowed and tried again. "How do you know as much as you do?"

He didn't speak.

"It isn't fair!" Although her clumsiness embarrassed her, and the butt plug poked uncomfortably, she managed a sitting position which caused the dildo and ropes to slide off. She couldn't bend her bound legs and had to lean forward to keep her balance. When she moved, they'd see the wet spot she'd deposited on the spread. "It isn't fair," she repeated. "You know everything about me but — "

"Not everything."

She stared at her pussy. "You know things about me no other man does. You understand my sexuality better than I do."

"True."

The simple acknowledgement made her shiver. "And

you remain an unknown."

"It's better this way."

"For whom?" she demanded although given her bonds, she was in no position to argue anything. "Ranger, I can't take any more."

"You're bailing?"

Hot. His simple statement became like fire pressed against her clit.

"You don't know what it's like. To be brought to the brink of climax over and over again..." Just thinking about what she'd endured caused her to break out in a sweat. "If I pass out—"

"You won't."

"How do you know?"

Instead of answering, he freed her legs. Now only her hands remained imprisoned. She tried to scoot to the edge of the bed, but he wouldn't let her. Resigned, she bent her knees, exposing her cunt.

"You aren't a woman, Ranger." Her voice sounded small, but with his hands only inches from her cunt, she couldn't help it. "You can't comprehend what it's like to have your clit stimulated over and over again—not allowed release."

"No." He picked up the dildo and pressed it against her nether lips. "I don't have a clit. But I've worked with enough of them."

Alarm shot through her. "Worked with? How many women have been in your life—have you done this to?"

She expected him to distract her by turning on the dildo, but he didn't. "You're talking about two things," he said. Then he stood and walked across the room.

She glanced at the discarded dildo, acknowledged the butt plug and leather on her wrists, her nakedness. "Two things," she whispered. "What do you mean?"

He turned around, and she easily read his tension and a vulnerability she hadn't seen before. For a moment he looked old and trapped, exquisitely vulnerable. For a heartbeat she loved him.

"I know how Scarlet Cavern operates because that's where I grew up."

Chapter Six

Shana couldn't have been more shocked if Ranger had confessed he was a wanted felon. Barely aware of what she was doing, she stood up. The plug remained where he'd placed it, and she couldn't use her hands, but she barely noticed either thing as she walked over to him. She all but tasted his tension.

"Get rid of the cuffs," she said.

"Nothing has changed. We're still doing this."

"I-I know. But for now…"

Gripping her arms more firmly than necessary, he turned her from him and undid the cuffs. Her mind in turmoil, she stayed where he'd positioned her. To her shock, he stroked the back of her neck. His gentle fingers transmitted emotions she needed but had never expected from him — tenderness and caring.

"What — ?" she started.

"This wasn't supposed to happen," he muttered. "Telling you what I just did — I never suspected I'd…"

"Then why did you?"

He stopped caressing, but because his fingers remained on her, she couldn't think. "Lean over," he said after a short telling silence, and she did so. She felt his hands separate her ass cheeks and grabbed her knees to balance herself. The moment he touched the plug, desire whipped through her. If only it was him, his cock! She'd never taken a man in her ass, but the thought of taking him that way caused her cheeks to flush. He slowly swirled the plug in a circle, then reversed direction. Her mouth sagged open. She couldn't remember how to swallow.

"My father taught me how to do this," he said, his tone rough. He pressed on the end and drove the hard intrusion deeper. "Everything I've learned about a woman's sexuality came from my old man."

Reacting to the cold pain in his voice, she straightened and turned to him. The plug served as an inescapable reminder of her sexuality. She felt like two separate entities, thinking woman and cunt.

"Your father?" she managed.

"Yeah. He started Scarlet Cavern."

"He what?"

"Founded it. Devised the concept."

"What-what about your mother?" she heard herself ask.

"I don't remember her."

A boy with no memories of the woman who'd given birth to him, a child raised in a perverted environment.

"Where—is your father still in charge? I'll be meeting him?" The thought horrified her. Was Ranger's father responsible for Lindsay's imprisonment?

He shook his head. "He sold it several years ago when he realized I wanted nothing to do with it. We were estranged when he died."

Lindsay, at least we don't have to deal with that. Lindsay, I'm trying-trying to get to you, but I'm in the middle of something – "You-you grew up surrounded by the-the lifestyle?"

"Yeah. Pretty abnormal, isn't it?"

"I, ah, I don't know."

"Diplomatic answer, I guess."

"What was it like?"

"The only childhood I knew. For years I didn't know there was anything else. And when I became a teenager, my cock ruled me. I turned into the proverbial kid in the candy store."

She didn't want to think of other women with him. "Was? What changed?"

He looked for all the world like a trapped animal. After everything he'd done to her, she should know better than to push him in any way. But she sensed they were approaching something he'd never shared with anyone, something that maybe explained his tender touch a few minutes ago. "I did."

"You grew up?"

"In a way. My old man said all the women we *recruited* wanted that lifestyle. I believed it, hell, I sucked into it for years because I never saw anything to the contrary, at least I didn't allow myself to see it. Then something happened."

The *something* was behind why he'd stopped having anything to do with his father. Believing she had no choice, she touched his chest. Beneath his shirt, she felt his heat, his beating heart. "What was it?" she whispered.

He made a move as if to pull her hands off him, then stopped. Staring down at her, he sighed. "Someone died."

Lindsay! Oh God. Please, be careful. "Who?"

"A woman who cried and pleaded and said she didn't want to be there."

She shuddered. "Why-why did you make her stay?"

"Not me. By then I was old enough to know most people didn't live their lives the way we did at Scarlet Cavern. I'd been exploring my own life, something normal."

"Normal?"

"Like I started tasting when my old man sent me to ranches to work during summer vacations and when I went to college." He put his hands on her buttocks and pulled her close. She didn't have to look down to know he was erect. "He wanted me to take over the *business* as he called it, telling me I couldn't turn my back on what had afforded me a damn good living and free education."

"He-he tried to make you feel guilty?"

"Oh yeah. He told me he didn't trust anyone else to continue his vision. That's what he called it, his vision. But I'd grown up watching him manipulate people. I refused to buy into it even though..."

"Even though what?" Their bodies were all but sealed together, her breasts flattened against him, his cock held between them.

"It's damn seductive, all right! Experiencing the ultimate in control and domination, although I knew some of the things that went on there were perverted, I loved being in charge, powerful."

Although she'd come willingly to him this time, she sensed his power. And hadn't he already demonstrated his ease in dominating her? "Did-did your father ever try to use that to get his way with you?"

His laugh was cold. He started running his fingers down her spine. She felt herself soften, resistance no longer a word she understood. Mindless to the danger, she wrapped her arms around his neck and held on.

"My old man was a master in every way. But finally his need to own killed a young woman."

"Oh God."

"The day I found her body, I called the cops and walked out the door. I didn't come back until after my father died."

Feeling as if she'd slipped into a swift-moving river, she tried to look into Ranger's eyes, but he held her too tight.

"You found her body?"

"Yeah. You don't want to hear this."

Of course she didn't, but want and need were two very different things. Ranger didn't resist when she led him back to the bed and pulled off his shirt. At any moment he could reassert his dominance, bind and silence her, but as long as he granted her freedom, she'd keep at him. He held her wrists when she unbuttoned and unzipped his jeans but did nothing to indicate he wanted her to stop. In truth, she sensed an element she hadn't expected to find in him — vulnerability. This powerful and gifted master of her sexuality wasn't immune to emotion after all. Beneath the masculine exterior beat the heart of a compassionate human being, a boy robbed of a normal upbringing. She couldn't give him back his childhood, but she could gift him with her own brand of compassion and with the act give them both what she know knew they needed. As for the emotional consequences...

By the time she'd taken away everything except his shorts, need zinged through her. If she worked it right, if she reached the need in him, they'd have sex.

But first...

Feeling no shame, she leaned over, reached behind her, and extracted the plug.

"You don't know how long she'd been there or under what circumstances she came to Scarlet Cavern?" she asked as she dropped the plug to the carpet.

"No. By then I had my own place." Ranger explained that the woman had been in what he called a control room when he'd reluctantly responded to his father's demand to come see him. The voluptuous woman had been presented to him as his reward for returning to the *fold*, but it hadn't taken him long to realize her terror was real. He insisted his father let her go, but the older man said he couldn't.

"Had he kidnapped her?"

"He refused to say and neither would anyone else there. The hell of it was, I didn't insist he free her the moment I laid eyes on her. By the time I sobered up and went looking for her, it was too late for her."

"Don't blame yourself. He was the guilty one."

"She's still dead. And although the case was prosecuted, my old man got off scot-free."

"And he lost what respect you had for him."

His flared nostrils served as the answer she needed. "I'm sorry," she managed. "People shouldn't feel that way about their parents."

"It's reality, a reality I've come to terms with."

She nodded, not just because she wanted to spare him further pain, but also because for the first time, the playing field between them had leveled. Yes, he still wore shorts, but he'd let her bring him this far. The final step was a given. As for after...

Forget after!

"I want to fuck you," she said as she took hold of the elastic band. "Only, *want* barely covers it. After what I've been forced to endure—"

"You got off on it. Almost."

"That's beside the point!" she shot back although he was right. "Building to something over and over again but never being allowed—" Awareness of how much she risked exposing by saying any more stopped her. Determined to turn things in the direction she needed, she pulled down and out on his shorts, accommodating the potent bulge. He could stop her, of course, but she didn't believe he would. Her heart needed more than primitive sex, but in the light of everything that had transpired between them and what lay ahead, the thought of telling him how much she'd come to care about him terrified her.

Crouching, she slid the fabric over his thighs, knees, calves. He stepped out of the last bit of clothing, but when she tried to straighten, he placed a hand on the top of her head and held her there.

She didn't care. What did equality matter as long as, finally, she fed her body's hunger? When he spread his legs slightly, she ran her fingers over his thighs, drawing out the exquisite moment when she touched his cock for the first time. Her heart beat erratically.

Soon, very soon, man and not something manmade would be housed in her.

Spurred on by the heady fantasy, she cupped her hands around what was precious to her. In her imagination she became a virgin touching a man's cock for the first time. A cock, often the object of women's jokes, was an incredible organ. Filled with blood and excitement, it was capable of creating the most exquisite experience.

As if painting it, she touched each inch of flesh, letting him know in every way possible that she'd long been dreaming of this moment. When he reduced her to helplessness and turned her body and mind against her, her thoughts had locked on the wonder of being speared by and on his cock, twitching under its power, melting and becoming whatever he wanted. In truth, feeling helpless under his penis' assault unnerved her, but she knew she wouldn't survive the alternative.

To live, truly live, she had to fuck him.

Strong and weak, she opened her mouth and drew the tip into her. In the past, she'd loved the feeling of control she got from performing this ritual, but although her teeth raked lightly over his velvet flesh, he was still the one in control. Not only did his strength outstrip hers, not only had he put foreign objects in her, not only did he hold the key to the room and chains, but whatever he'd done to her had turned her from modern civilized woman into a she-animal in heat.

However he wanted it, as many times as he wanted, she'd spread her lips and legs for him and live for the invasion.

Invasion! His cock filling her mouth and leaving no space for speech. His very maleness sliding over and into her, stripping her mind and turning her primitive.

Lost in conflicting thoughts and emotions, she tried to focus on what she was doing, but as she slowly brought more and more of his cock into her mouth, the act was all instinct.

He'd laced his fingers in her hair and held her, monitoring her every move, not quite trusting her. She should laugh. After everything he'd done to her, eating him was nothing. Still, if she wanted, she could turn her teeth into weapons and punish him, teach him a lesson.

She didn't want.

Driven by the pulsing heat in her pussy, she stumbled to her feet and pushed him onto the bed. He landed on his back with his legs dangling over the side. Much as she wanted to join him, for a moment she simply savored the view. *You're incredible! The answer to dreams I never knew I had, heart and body rolled into one, layers of complexity, strength and weakness.*

"What are you thinking?" he demanded.

"What? That it's my turn," she said.

"This time it is."

This time. Then there'd be others? Unable to look beyond this moment, she scrambled onto the bed and straddled him. She perched over his hips with his cock in front of her. It glistened with her saliva. She'd always needed a measure of foreplay to prepare her body for intercourse, but not this time. During the seemingly countless times when he'd played her, he'd found a sexual trigger she didn't know she possessed. Now, it seemed, even self-preservation came second to her need, her instinct, for sex.

Resigned and half-crazed with wanting at the same time, she positioned herself over his cock and directed it at her pussy. Feeling as if she'd finally come home, she pulled her lips aside and settled on him. He slid in, claimed her, shared his flesh with hers.

He clamped his hands over her hips and held her in place. Once he'd asserted his command, he bent his knees, braced his feet against the mattress and began driving into her. Mouth open to bring enough air into her lungs, she met him thrust for thrust. Sweat pooled under her breasts and at the small of her back. His cock worked piston-like inside her flooded opening, and she began moaning in time with the heated electricity pulsing through her. He'd turned her into fire, pushed her to the top of a mountain. She stood poised at the peak, not caring whether she flew or fell.

Her moans grew and quickened. She pounded into him, held nothing back. She could swallow his cock with her cunt, claim it as her own, house it in her for the rest of her life.

"I'm coming! Coming!" she screamed when her cunt muscles began contracting.

"Let go! Let go!"

She did, screaming loud and long. The contractions came one after another so fast she couldn't separate them. They built, intensified, turned hot. And she kept screaming.

Chapter Seven

"Get up."

Barely aware of her surroundings, Shana fought past sleep. The moment cool air brushed her naked breasts, she remembered why she was here, what Ranger had done to her since her arrival. Mostly her thoughts settled on the wild sex they'd shared.

"Someone's on his way. Before he gets here, I want to prepare you."

Last night—at least she thought it had been last night—Ranger's voice had been husky with desire, but now it held no warmth. Hurt and alarmed, she rubbed her eyes and focused on him. He wore his usual uniform of jeans and pullover shirt and was barefoot. His hair was wet, and he smelled like soap, making her wish they'd showered together. A few days ago she hadn't known he existed. Now he was the most important person in her life—maybe the only one.

"Who's coming?" she asked.

The question earned her a sharp slap on the butt cheek. She tried to scoot away, but he grabbed her ankle and yanked her toward him. She considered kicking him, but this was the man who'd put an end to unbelievable sexual tension. Besides, she hadn't forgotten what he'd told her about his growing up without a mother and the vulnerability he'd revealed.

"Bathroom," he ordered as he hauled her to her feet.

"What is it?" she demanded. "Why are you acting this way?"

"We crossed a line last night," he said without looking at her. "It won't happen again."

"Why not?" She hated sounding desperate but no way could she rein in her emotions. "What was wrong about what we did?"

"Everything." He pressed his hand over his eyes. When she could again see them, she recognized something she hadn't expected. He was haunted.

"We can talk about it," she suggested. "We have to."

"No. We don't," he insisted and shoved her toward the bathroom.

He joined her in the small room, and as she relieved herself, he turned on the shower. Delighted by the thought of getting clean and having the opportunity to clear her thinking, she started to step in.

"Not so fast. Hands behind you."

"What?"

"Didn't you hear me?" He slapped her ass. "Hands where I say."

What had happened to the lover she'd taken into her? Off-balance and a little frightened, she did as he ordered. He roped her wrists together then wrapped several lengths of rope around her waist. Finally, he secured her hands at the small of her back.

"In," he ordered. "And if you say a word, I'll gag you."

Either way she'd lose. Desperately needing to understand the change in him, she stepped under the spray. He grabbed her neck and held her so the water ran over her hair. Once it was thoroughly wet, he pulled her close and shampooed her hair. He made no attempt to keep the shampoo out of her eyes, forcing her to close them. There was nothing gentle in the way he handled her as he rinsed her hair. He'd soaped a washcloth and had started scrubbing her before she dared open her eyes.

He stood outside the shower but water had soaked his shirt. As a child, she'd raised several calves as 4-H projects. Ranger's handling of her reminded her of the quick, efficient way she'd bathed her animals before a competition. When he forced her to lean forward and briskly rubbed her butt and pubic area, she felt less than human, a piece of flesh he was preparing for...for what?

He hauled her out. She tried to stand immobile, but when he scrubbed at her breasts with a towel, she whimpered and stumbled away. Unfortunately, she ran into the shower stall.

"You aren't going anywhere," he informed her. "I have a hell of a lot to do and not much time. Turn around and lean forward."

She did so dutifully but not being able to use her hands made keeping her balance difficult. Fortunately, maybe, he wanted her to spread her legs.

The calves she'd raised had eventually been bought by various grocery stores. She hated thinking about animals she'd spent countless hours tending to going to the slaughterhouse, but with Ranger handling her as if she was a side of beef, she had no choice. He ran the towel between her legs and pulled the terrycloth back and forth, irritating flesh still sensitive from yesterday.

"You're hurting—" she started, then forced herself to shut up. She thought he might punish her for her outburst, but he only continued rubbing her pussy, maybe branding it.

"Better," he said. He spun her around, and she looked up at him. This was an imposing stranger, not the vulnerable man he'd revealed in the night. He spread his fingers over her hips, digging in so she could barely think of anything else. "What happened between us earlier was a mistake," he said through clenched teeth. "It won't happen again."

Why not? What are you afraid of? Instead of asking, she nodded in acknowledgement.

"I told you things I never thought I would," he continued. "Things I shouldn't have. And it was too soon for you to be anything except sexually frustrated. Now — " He leaned close. "I have to start over."

"Why? Ranger, all I want is to find Lindsay." she said when her friend's safety had become part of something much larger. "What does how it happens matter?"

"Because this is the only way you'll understand, the way I know."

* * * * *

Shana hoped he'd feed her, but he obviously didn't care that last night's gymnastics had made her hungry. Once he'd run a brush through her hair, he hauled her back into the training room. She couldn't keep her eyes off the dresser with its seemingly endless toys. Only when he positioned her in front of it did she notice he'd put a thin mattress on the floor. He hooked his foot around her ankle and jerked. Knocked off her feet, she landed on her knees on the mattress. He dropped beside her then forced her onto her belly.

In that silent way of his, he knelt near her hips and pulled her ass cheeks apart. She tried to get on her side, but he easily held her in place. "A little fighting is good, Shana. Fighting gives each of us a goal. But although I understand your resistance, it won't do you any good."

"You don't own me!"

"We've gone too far, Shana. I know you don't want out."

"No, damn it," she admitted. "I don't. I can't leave now."

Something long and hard and cold was being pressed against her anus. Afraid he intended to shove what had to be a rod in her, she fought with all her strength. Perhaps taunting her, he slid the length between her buttocks and held it in place. She renewed her efforts. With a grunt, he gently straddled her lower back facing her feet.

"I told you." He slapped her buttocks repeated, one cheek at a time. "You aren't going to win this battle." To her horror and disgust, he slid the rod back and forth in a gesture that mirrored what he'd done with the towel but didn't insert it. Beyond all reason, in her mind the rod became his cock. Her muscles tightened around the foreign object.

He ran a finger over her pussy. "Getting your attention, am I? Well, if I wasn't under a time constraint, we could wrestle until you run out of gas. However —" He fingered her again, careful not to disturb the rod resting along her crease. "We have a lot of ground to cover and not much time."

She shivered and struggled when he looped rope over her ankles, but of course like every other time, he won this battle. When he'd finished, her ankles were crossed and snugly held in place. To emphasize what she already knew, he tugged on the bonds.

"My letting you kick me is counter-productive. Besides, if you managed to connect and knock me out, you'd just have to hang around until I came too. And I'd be mad. You don't want me mad."

She still harbored fantasies of landing blow after blow where it would do the most good, but when he grabbed the ankle ropes and straightened her on the pitiful excuse for a mattress, she didn't try to fight. From what she could tell, the rod was about two feet long. It effectively held her attention—and more. If only she could anticipate what he had in mind, it...

The thought ended when he tugged on the ankle rope. Turning, she realized he was securing her ankles to the foot of the bed. Great! Now she couldn't as much wriggle away. *This is for you, Lindsay. You're going to owe me so —*

No, not just Lindsay.

"Helplessness is an endless process," he explained conversationally. "Different people react in different ways, but one thing I learned at my old man's elbow—no one remains unaffected. I gave you a taste of it yesterday, but by the time I'm done with you, you won't remember what having ownership of your body feels like."

He took hold of her wrists and pulled them as far from her body as the waist rope allowed. "And because I know what I'm doing, you'll be happy to have me take over." She couldn't tell what he was doing to her wrists but thought he was adding yet more rope. "I bring pleasure, Shana. Pleasure your friend has become addicted to. Outsiders might call it forced pleasure, but after all the lessons are learned, you won't see it that way. In fact—"

He stood and stepped toward the head of the bed. Feeling yet another tug in her arms, she turned her head toward him. He held rope connected to her wrists. "In fact—" He looped the rope around the metal headboard and tightened it. "The time will come when you'll get down on your knees and beg me to claim you. Then when you and Lindsay get together, you'll be speaking the same language. It's what you want from me, what I intend to give you. The only thing."

"Only?" she whimpered. "Last night—"

"Forget last night!" he ordered. His eyes burned.

Stretched and unmoving, she thought back to her first rodeo because he was right; although she'd do anything to help him heal from his childhood, she wanted nothing to do with memories of fucking him, caring about him. A steer had been released, but as soon as it began running, two cowboys on horseback with lassoes galloped after the terrified animal. In a matter of seconds, all four of the steer's legs had been lassoed, and it lay heaving in the dust. She'd become that creature. *And more. So much more.*

"You don't need this anymore," Ranger told her as he drew the rod out. With her breasts mashed against the mattress, and her upper body all but held in a vise, she caught only glimpses of him when he came near her head. For the most part, she was reduced to staring at the mattress and straining to anticipate his next movement. He went back to the drawer and pulled something out. Then he plugged it into a wall socket. Then a buzzing sound started. Unnerved, she fought her ropes.

"Enough!" Ranger pressed down on her back. "You're just going to wear yourself out."

She stopped struggling and chewed on her lower lip.

Although she was more than a little afraid, in truth, she was also looking forward to what he planned to do to her. There were lessons and then there were lessons, after all. And the things he'd proven himself capable of...

"Damn you!" she spluttered when he began slapping her buttocks again.

No way was there anything erotic about this. Instead, he struck her repeatedly as a housewife might beat the dust out of an old carpet. Her flesh became more and more sensitive; she imagined her ass growing red and hoped to hell his hand was getting sore. The buzzing sound went on and on, lulling her nearly to sleep. She might have drifted off if not for the unrelenting semi-punishment.

Finally he stopped. She exhaled into the mattress, waited.

"Do you understand the process?" he asked.

"The...process."

"Of how your priorities are being changed. You're becoming more—shall we say?—carnal. You haven't eaten today. What's more important to you? Getting fed or getting fucked?"

"I'm not—"

"Which?" He punctuated his question by slipping something hard between her pelvis and the mattress. The something, her body immediately informed her, had been responsible for the vibrating sound. Not particularly thick, the object ended in a series of knobby protrusions that rested a millimeter from her clit. Instead of being hard extensions of the vibrator's base, they retained a certain flexibility. As a result, each nub sent off its own humming message.

"Food or finding out how long it takes this little toy to

send you into the next world."

So close to her clit! Waves of sensation spreading throughout her, electrifying what was already highly charged!

"Which?" He spun the instrument in a rocking motion. "Want some cereal, Shana? Maybe bacon and an omelet."

"I...don't care!"

"Oh, I think you do." He freed her ankles from the bed while still keeping his so-called toy in place. "Look at that, Shana. You don't have to stay in one position after all. True, the ropes on your hands limit your possibilities, but if you want, you can scoot your ass away from me." He stroked her buttocks. "Your choice. Get away or stay."

Her mouth had gone numb. Her eyes felt as if they were bulging, and she imagined her nose wide and flaring as she struggled to bring in enough oxygen. Her ankles remained tied together, but Ranger was right. She could wriggle away on her belly. *Or stay.*

Beyond caring about dignity, she tucked her knees under her and pushed her buttocks into the air. She separated her legs as much as possible in a desperate attempt to increase his access to her. Much of her weight rested on her shoulders, and although her head was turned in his direction, she couldn't see him.

"Do me, please!" she sobbed.

Saying nothing, he repositioned the toy between her legs and angled it so the nubs were centered over and around her clit. Wild for satisfaction, she silently begged him to press into her. Instead, the man who obviously knew more about her sexual responses than she did barely touched her—at least there. He cupped his free hand around her closest breast and flattened it against her.

"Feel it," he whispered. "This is something that was designed at the Cavern." He too-briefly increased the pressure on her aching clit then backed off. "They call it the master or Master for short. That's because the women lucky enough to have it used on them agree their pussies become slaves to it."

In another place or time she would have argued that no modern woman would let an electrical apparatus rule them, but not only was she in no position to disagree, she wanted — *needed* — to be mastered.

"Do me!" she begged. "Please!"

"So, how's it going?" a strange male voice asked.

Chapter Eight

Ranger had been expecting Damek Whitset and shouldn't have been surprised that the current CEO of Scarlet Cavern hadn't bothered to knock. But although Damek held majority interest in the house Ranger had brought Shana to and had his own set of keys, he resented the intrusion.

"She's getting there," he said and reluctantly turned off the Master. "In fact she's coming along faster than I thought."

"You seem to be enjoying yourself." Damek indicated Ranger's erection. "So, are you going to introduce us?"

What he wanted was to order the heavy-set man in his fifties to get the hell out of here so he could give Shana what she needed, deserved, and had earned, but without Damek's approval, Shana would never see the inside of the Cavern or her friend, a reality he didn't dare forget.

Shana had collapsed on the mattress and was trying to look back at Damek. Ranger made things easier for her by freeing her hands from the bed. He left the ropes on her wrists and used the loops around her waist to help her sit up. Her gaze went from him to Damek, then back on him again. He read her confusion, embarrassment, and still-hot sexual excitement.

It was you and me last night, he thought. *My opening up to you in a way I never believed possible. I don't know why it happened. That's why I'm acting the way I am today, being a bastard. I have to keep you at arms' length; do you understand?*

Otherwise-otherwise you'll find the real me, and I'm scared to have that happen.

Damek stepped over and hauled Shana to her feet. Then he stepped back and gave her an appraising look. "Fine-looking piece of merchandise. So, miss, you're interested in the lifestyle, are you?"

"The...lifestyle?"

"Maybe that isn't what Ranger calls it. After all, he's been — how should we say it? — in retirement for several years. But when he said he was working with a new recruit and asked to use the place, I decided to have a look."

Dismissing Shana, Damek turned his attention on Ranger. "What's going on?"

He'd known Damek wouldn't easily buy into his story about renewed interest in the Cavern's lifestyle now his father was dead. Although he didn't mind lying for his own sake, things had changed since he'd spent time with Shana. She was no longer just a paycheck. She'd become — what?

"I told you," he said. The Master dangled from his fingers. "She isn't sure she's interested in the scene so wanted a preview. She came looking for me."

"Looking for you? What about it, miss? How'd you hear about Ranger?"

"From...a friend."

"What friend?"

"I'm not going to give you her name!" Shana shot back. "What I will tell you is she was, ah, associated with Scarlet Cavern back when Ranger's father was in charge."

That got Damek's attention. "I see," he said.

"Yes. My friend… I spent the weekend at her house and found some pictures she'd had taken of her at Scarlet Cavern. I wasn't shocked. I was…intrigued."

For a woman who smelled pungently of her own juices, Shana was doing a remarkable job of thinking on her feet. Wondering how she'd react, he tapped the Master against his thigh. She ignored him.

"The pictures, well, they walked a thin line between consent and coercion. I wanted to explore the possibilities, but I didn't want to be hurt."

"From the looks of your ass, Ranger has been less than gentle."

Shrugging, Shana turned so he and Damek had a clear view of her buttocks. "No, he hasn't, but I'm not suing. In fact, if you hadn't shown up…"

"You'd be screaming about now."

"Hopefully." She spun back around. "My friend said Ranger's father respected the merchandise, and his son abided by the same—how should I call it?—work ethic. I thought, well, I thought I'd be safer with an older man, but when I learned he'd died, I went looking for the son."

"Ranger hasn't wanted to be found for several years."

"Tell me about it," Shana said with a laugh. "I had to hire a private detective. And it took a bit to convince him to work with me, but we hammered out an arrangement."

"Hmm. And what's your goal, miss? When he's done with you, what do you intend to do with your newfound wisdom?"

The way Shana stood up to Damek, Ranger had trouble remembering that her hands were still tied. As for her nudity, he hadn't come close to dismissing that.

"I haven't decided. I was hoping today's-today's lesson would help."

"The S&M scene? You thinking of taking the plunge?"

"Maybe. Unless I decide to take my services to Scarlet Cavern."

Damek laughed long and loud. Then shaking his head in obvious admiration, he approached Shana and kissed her on the cheek. "It could be a lucrative decision on your part. I'm sure we'll make room for you. You're beautiful."

"Thanks. I work at it. I've done some modeling. I understand the camera."

"Put that on your resume."

"Then you'll accept one from me?"

"Oh yeah."

Gaining access to Scarlet Cavern had always been Shana's goal. But instead of feeling as if he'd fulfilled his contract with her, Ranger would do anything to keep her as far from that place as possible. Or would he? Damn it, he didn't own her, not really. She was free to do whatever she wanted, what she believed she needed to accomplish.

"What do you think, Ranger?" Damek asked. "Is she ready to give us a demonstration? From the looks and smell of her, I'd say so."

"A demonstration?" Shana asked.

"It could be a continuation of what I interrupted although I'd prefer something more visual." Still smiling, Damek indicated the Master. "It's the perfect instrument, but a woman with her pussy hugging the ground might as well be invisible. What about it? Shall we call this your audition? If I judge you worthy, you can start making some serious money."

"What-what do I have to do?"

"Ah, a little hesitancy. Good. The paying customers don't like a jaded model." Acting as if he had every right to her, Damek grabbed hold of Shana's nipple and briskly rubbed it. "There's a lot of things people can fake in this world, but contrary to the acting that goes on in countless bedrooms, the camera knows the difference between fake and real orgasms. What about it, Ranger? Has she produced the real thing?"

With me in her. "Yeah," he acknowledged when it took all his self-control not to deck Damek.

"I thought so." Damek released Shana's nipple. "Hard as a rock. Damn but I love a responsive boob. Speaking of responsive—" He ran his hand between Shana's legs and pushed up, forcing a gasp from her. She started to step back, then stopped.

"Watch it," Ranger warned. "She isn't a piece of merchandise."

"Maybe. Maybe not. What about it, miss?" Damek continued the intimate assault. "You ready to be seen as merchandise by thousands of horny men?"

"To-to have pictures taken?"

"A whole damn movie."

"At Scarlet Cavern?"

"Where else?"

Don't do it, Ranger warned with his eyes.

I have to, she responded as he knew she would.

You're the bravest woman I've ever known. Putting your friend ahead of yourself— no one's ever done that for me. No one ever cared enough.

* * * * *

Shana fervently hoped they'd gag her, but although she was afraid of what she might say once they started in on her, they didn't cut off her ability to talk. While she talked to Damek, Ranger's eyes had been alive with warning, but now she couldn't begin to read his expression.

And as soon as Damek backed her up to the metal footboard, she stopped trying. Damek retied her. Although her arms were still behind her, he'd gotten rid of the waist restraint and had fastened her elbows close together. Then he positioned her hands on the mattress and leaned her as far back as the footboard allowed. He next fastened her wrists to the headboard so she couldn't straighten. As if she wasn't already helpless, he ordered her to spread her legs and secured her ankles to the bottom of the bed. He took more unnecessary steps by fastening her calves and thighs in the same way. Although she couldn't look down at herself, she knew her cunt was fully exposed.

Through all this, all Ranger did was supply Damek with the necessary ropes.

"That was fun," Damek said. "In my executive position, I too seldom get to do any on-hands work. However, much as I relish completing the experiment, from now on, I'd rather watch. Ranger?"

At the moment, Ranger stood across the room, leaning against the wall and looking disinterested. Or she would have believed he didn't care if not for his far from discrete erection and clenched fists. She couldn't decide which meant the most to her.

"You don't have to do this, Shana," he said.

Yes I do. Otherwise I might never see Lindsay again. "I'm looking forward to it." Her throat was so dry she couldn't swallow.

"Are you?" Damek asked. "Either you were already horny when Ranger started educating you, or you've been a receptive student. Of course he is extraordinarily skilled in this-this business. There's been none better."

"Stop it," Ranger warned.

"Don't play modest with me," Damek shot back with a note of authority she hadn't heard before. "Shana, the other so-called doms increased their skills tenfold from watching his work. We never could get him to teach lessons, but seeing him in action is all it takes. Your skills aren't rusty, are they, Ranger? Going by what's glistening on the lady's lips, I don't think so."

Maybe she should have been embarrassed at having her arousal pointed out, but she could barely concentrate on the words. Damek had gone to the dresser and was taking a video camera out of a case.

"What's that for?" she asked.

"Marketing," Damek replied. "Surely you understand that's a major part of what makes the Cavern successful. Granted, the lighting here isn't the best, but the camera is state of the art." He positioned himself in front of her and aimed the lens at her crotch. She struggled to close her legs, but of course she couldn't.

"I forbid—"

"Too late." Damek chuckled. "You've been a willing participant in the proceedings so far, haven't you?"

Thinking of the thin line between consent and being overwhelmed, she stared at Ranger. He didn't acknowledge her.

Did I imagine last night? Not the sex of course; that was real. But believing you cared about me — was it an act on your part?

If so she was deeply grateful she hadn't told him she'd briefly loved him.

"No denial, my dear?" Damek pushed a button on the camera and a faint whirring sound started. He stepped to the right then crouched, changing the lens' angle. "At the Cavern, we provide the subs — mostly women — with the means of fulfilling their fantasies. But instead of charging for our services," he chuckled, "the subs are compensated handsomely for their acting skills. Although it isn't acting, is it? Ranger, you're ready to begin?"

Begin? Wasn't being helpless enough?

She thought she'd scream when Ranger crawled onto the bed and knelt behind her. Then he ran his hands over her shoulders and gently cupped her breasts, and fear died. He cradled her against his chest as he began a sensuous massage. In a matter of seconds, her nipples hardened and heated. Despite the strain in her back, she'd be content to stay like this for as long as he was here, doing this, tending to her, embracing her, his hands loving her.

Maybe she should have been forewarned when he took hold of her nipples and drew up on them, but all she could think about was his chest's warmth and his breath on her naked flesh — feeling his touch again. His grip grew stronger, harsher. She sucked in a breath and tried to read his expression, but his face was so close, she saw only a blurred outline.

"What are you doing?" she managed.

"Testing your limits."

My limits for what? In a dim way she realized Damek stood close by as he recorded Ranger's manipulations.

Ranger ran a hand over her belly and hips. The other hand remained locked on her breasts, forcing her to try to concentrate on two things at once. Although she could barely wait for him to reach the juncture of her legs, she still jumped and gasped when he slid his expert fingers between her labia. He briefly stroked her clit then left it alone and deprived.

His chest pressed hard against her backward-thrust shoulders, a position that brought his thighs in contact with her bound arms. Even as he played at the entrance to her cunt, her arms recorded the feel of his erection through the jeans she'd come to hate.

You, me, alone together again, please! My heart — you've done something to it I don't understand any more than I can control my physical responses.

"What are you — what are you going to do?" she managed.

"Whatever I damn well want and you're going to take it."

Biting back a sob, she struggled against panic. Then it dawned on her that he was playing to the camera, and she hated him for scaring her. But even knowing his harshness was part of an act didn't silence her unease. How could it be otherwise when she'd been rendered helpless — when the man in charge of her body knew its strengths and weaknesses so well?

"She's into pain?" Damek asked.

"Moderate."

"Show me."

"Damn it! Don't tell me — "

"Yeah, I will. Otherwise, she'll never see the inside of the Cavern. What about it, bitch? You willing to pay your dues?"

Chapter Nine

Ranger had gotten off the bed and dropped to his knees in front of her unmoving body, but although she should be trying to anticipate, all Shana could think about were her last words. *Yes*, she'd told Damek. She was ready to pay her dues.

This better be worth it, Lindsay. If I've gotten myself into this over nothing, I'll never forgive you.

She was trying to come up with an appropriate punishment for her friend — probably because she needed to have her mind on anything except what might come next — when something cold and hard touched her opening. She jumped and rose on tiptoe — the only movement afforded her.

"What — ?" she began.

"A toy," Damek supplied. "Why don't I describe it to you? There's a small nub that'll go in you but not far, hardly a fraction of what a cock's capable of. What's interesting about the design is the way the metal cups a woman's pussy kind of like a small blanket."

"Metal?" she managed. Ranger was placing what felt like an elastic strap low around her waist. The elastic held the top of the hard cup against her privates. She was still trying to comfort herself with the thought that she could at least shake it loose when Ranger reached between her legs and fastened yet another strap in place. This one secured the bottom of the cup to her. She could feel the nub Damek had mentioned. He was right; it barely invaded. But what unnerved her was how the whole thing settled securely over her cunt and pressed against her clit. Trying to make sense of it, she tightened her pelvis muscles. She couldn't possibly free herself. "Why metal?" she asked on a sigh.

"You'll see, you'll see." Damek's tone was both teasing and aroused. "You haven't charged her yet, have you?" he asked Ranger.

"I told you I haven't."

"Just asking. You've been in retirement too long, lost your edge, your ability to disassociate yourself from the sub."

"Go to hell."

"Probably. Fuck it, Ranger, I'm not stupid. Your cock's about to burst. That never used to happen."

She could appeal to Ranger, order him to tell her what he had in mind and demand he forget the whole damn thing. But the truth was, not only hadn't her commitment to Lindsay not changed, she wanted to experience whatever Ranger had in mind.

"This is going to take awhile," Ranger said. "And she'll lose circulation in her arms if I keep them like they are."

"What do you have in mind?" Damek sounded dubious.

"Putting her on the bed."

Without so much as acknowledging her, the men set about untying her. When she could straighten, she concentrated on rubbing the circulation back into her arms. Then, not sure she wanted to, she looked down at herself. The object Ranger had fastened over her was black and curved to her contours, maybe four inches wide and twice as long. Electrical line led from it to a tissue-sized box on the floor. Heart hammering, she fingered the elastic straps.

"Don't ask," Damek ordered as if reading her mind, "because we're not going to tell you what it's capable of. Anticipation and enjoyment should be ends in themselves."

Ranger picked up the box and hauled her around to the side of the bed. She could barely walk with that—that thing on her. Not that she'd admit it of course, but the way the nub brushed against her inner lips felt wonderful. If things didn't get any worse...

Without so much as a please, Ranger picked her up and threw her onto the bed on her back. He placed the box between her legs, then walked around to the head of the bed and ordered her to stretch her arms back toward him.

She didn't want to do this! She didn't! Still, she did as he'd commanded, barely caring when he cuffed her wrists to one of the bars in the headboard. Her elbows and upper arms restricted her ability to see to the sides.

"You don't need help, do you?" Damek asked. "A pro like you is used to working solo."

Ranger didn't acknowledge the question. Instead, as Damek started filming again, he positioned her legs wide apart and secured them at the ankles, knees, and thighs so she could do little more than wiggle her toes. When he'd finished, he leaned close and kissed her navel. Undone by the gesture, she struggled to lift her hips toward him.

"Remember what I said at the beginning," he muttered. "If you want out, just say so."

"You-you'll be here?"

"Yes." His eyes met hers.

"Then so am I," she whispered.

A look she interpreted as wonder passed over him. He kissed her again and pressed his damp tongue into her navel. Then, although she wondered if she might have died for him at this moment, he straightened and stepped away from the bed.

"Ranger?" Her voice sounded small.

"She has beautiful breasts," Damek said. "But they're naked."

"Is that an order?"

"Yeah." Damek chuckled. "You got it."

From out of the corner of her eye, she saw Damek coming closer, the lens panning over her spread and helpless body. Although she hated giving him what he wanted, she couldn't keep her apprehension to herself.

Because she'd been concentrating on the older man, she was slow to realize Ranger had positioned himself on the other side of the bed. She turned toward him and tried to flatten her arm so she could see him better. He'd taken her so many places, got closer to her than any man ever had; the intimacies bonded them and not just for today.

The nipple clips he placed on her breasts felt small, almost delicate. They went on effortlessly, but she gasped as sudden pain spread over her breasts. Fortunately, it faded, leaving only a tingling throb. Not until he picked up the slender chain between the clips and tugged on it did she comprehend fully what he'd accomplished.

Much as she longed to beg the men to tell her what was coming next, she remained silent. If she didn't speak, didn't interact, maybe she could remain remote and aloof.

Aloof? Hardly.

"Is she a screamer?" Damek asked.

Ranger didn't answer, and although she hated herself for her weakness, she began shaking. *I trust you, Ranger. Maybe I'm crazy, but I trust you.*

"She looks like a screamer," Damek continued, his tone both aroused and seductive. "What about it, Shana? What are you like when you climax? Ladylike or a hellion?"

"Shut the fuck up!" Ranger ordered.

Damek grunted. "The man speaks. You've got it bad, don't you? I've never seen you care like this before."

Care? Ranger, what is he talking about?

"I'm just doing my job," Ranger barked. "And I don't appreciate you playing to the video. Do your damn filming, will you?"

She should try to comprehend the animosity between the men, but thinking about anything except her body, specifically her sex organs, was impossible. Damek had inadvertently hit on something though. Much as she enjoyed a good climax, she'd always been unnerved by her lack of self-control. When she climaxed, she screamed. Hell, at the moment she felt in heat, insatiable.

Would it be like that today?

What do you think? Remember last night?

The pussy-cup began vibrating. Alarmed, she tried but of course failed to sit up. She felt sweat form in her armpits. Determined to remain on top of things, she started counting silently. She'd gotten no further than ten when the vibrations kicked up a notch. But it wasn't just humming. An electrical current...

"No! Stop! What are you doing?"

"A gift," Damek informed her. "One hell of a gift."

Focusing was becoming difficult. She concentrated on Ranger. He held the control box, his fingers on the knobs. "Slow buildup," he said dispassionately. "All that energy concentrated on your clit."

One of the videos of Lindsay had shown her chained to a wall with her legs forced apart, something Shana didn't recognize fastened to her pussy. Although she'd only been able to watch a few seconds of the horrid scene, she again heard her friend's rapid-fire groans and sobs. Lindsay had tugged at her bonds, her attention focused on the masked man torturing her.

Torture. Forced climax.

"I — stop! I insist you — stop!"

"Too late," Damek informed her. "Hang in there 'cause in a moment, stopping will be the last thing you'll want."

Thinking to tell Ranger how afraid she was, she struggled to turn toward him. But as she did, the electrical charge increased again and stole her attention. Nothing mattered except experiencing, trying to anticipate, comprehending. Another notch, she swore the current now extended from belly to knees. Most of the energy was concentrated on her clit all right. She swore it was expanding, heating.

She started moaning, her hips sliding to and fro in a disorganized attempt to absorb the energy. Sweat pooled between her breasts. More sweat ran down her sides; her throat felt on fire. Her body became a puppet manipulated by a mechanical master. Her cunt muscles contracted, released, contracted again.

Higher, stronger, all-consuming.

"Do, do, do," she chanted. "Oh God, let me! Let me!"

"Beg for it, Shana!" Damek ordered. "Beg."

"Please!" Her buttocks burned from rubbing against the sheet, but she couldn't hold still. "Please!"

"Please what?"

"Fuck-fuck me!"

To her horror, the charge decreased, bringing her back from the brink. Drenched in sweat and wild with frustration, she blinked back tears and glared at Ranger. He'd become a stranger, a dark and remote stranger devoid of the humanity she'd found last night. "What are you doing?" she demanded. She sounded like a begging child.

"You don't want this."

"Yes I do!"

"It'll change you," he said while a soft current buzzed through her. "You can't go back after this."

Back to what? It was already too late.

"I don't care! I've—I think I've waited my whole life for this."

"If you get it, you'll spend the rest of your life needing more."

His hard truth terrified her. Yet, helpless and alive in a way she'd never believed possible, she knew it was already too late. "I don't care. I've never felt more alive."

Leaning close, he stroked her inner thighs. "Men are ruled by their cocks. Slaves to them. Do you want the same?"

"Yes. Yes."

"When the hell are you going to—?" Damek started,

but Ranger silenced him with a curse.

"Ranger, please," she whimpered. "I've always needed—something I've never found. This is it. I know it is."

He didn't respond but continued to caress her flesh. Far from being embarrassed because she lay spread and dripping beneath him, she felt safe in a way she'd hadn't known was possible. This man could be both cruel and gentle, and wrapped in that package was compassion and caring—maybe something more.

"I trust you," she whispered. "I turn my body over to you."

She felt like exploding when he leaned down and kissed what of her mons wasn't covered by the electrical conduit. Then he turned his attention back to the box.

More energy, more challenge and life.

Although she'd been on this journey before, she felt new. Her pussy was being more than tickled. Light fingers danced over it in ever-increasing waves. The waves spread outward and touched every part of her.

As the sensation between her legs increased, she felt her essence being tunneled down until nothing else mattered. She longed to drink of her own juices, to bury her fingers in her so she could feel the vibrations. Her vaginal muscles contracted in spasmic waves she couldn't begin to control.

She dimly felt her breasts swell, felt the bite of metal on her nipples. Something pulled on them. Despite her hazed world, she realized Ranger had taken hold of the chain. He continued to manipulate the box, forcing more and more power into it.

She began bucking like a trapped animal, made

mewling sounds that went on and on. Lightheaded, she sucked in hot air and tried to close her mouth. She couldn't. Instead she screamed and screamed and screamed.

Fire burst between her legs. Lightning licked at her cunt lips. Her clit all but exploded in a thunderclap of sensation. If it hadn't been for her bonds, she would have folded in on herself — either that or taken flight.

No. Neither of those things. If she was free, she knew she'd wrap herself around Ranger.

"Oh god, god, god!" she chanted.

Then her violent climax slammed into her, and she knew nothing.

Chapter Ten

"Shit," Damek muttered. "Shit."

Ranger tucked the blanket around Shana's shoulders and stared down at the sleeping or unconscious woman. She'd want a shower and food when she woke up, but he didn't expect that to happen for several hours. He could still feel her heat. Her damp hair clung to her forehead and the sides of her neck, and he thought her beautiful.

He'd given her the gift she'd begged for and for a few minutes had deluded himself into believing only he understood her body enough to bring her the greatest pleasure, but of course that was a lie. Any educated dom could get her to dance and climax, and that's all he was to her — a manager of sex tools.

What is this, Ranger? Feeling sorry for yourself?

"That's Academy Award performance," Damek said as he put the video camera back in its case. "Talk about going off! What I wouldn't give to have her in my bed."

"Shut the fuck up." Feeling more than a little ill, Ranger returned the Pussy Probe, cuffs, and ropes to the dresser.

"What the hell's your problem?" Damek demanded. "Look, you want a compliment, I'll give you one. This bitch is one hell of a find."

Ranger whirled on the man who was nearly old enough to be his father. "Don't call her a bitch!"

"She couldn't be more in heat if she was a dog."

If he said anything, he'd probably also slug Damek. Not only would the man charge him with assault, but he'd have screwed any chance he had of getting Shana into the Cavern. Of course if he was dismissed, Damek would be more than happy to act as Shana's go-between. Whatever it took, he wouldn't leave her alone in there, wouldn't let her go in without him.

After insisting they leave Shana alone, he made two stiff drinks. He downed his in three gulps and mixed another before he felt calm enough to carry on a conversation. Although Damek was still agitated over Shana's violent climax, Ranger insisted on focusing on business. He had no trouble getting Damek to admit he could hardly wait for Shana to join the Cavern's stable and made an appointment to bring her there in three days.

Damek tried to talk him into their showing up earlier, but he held off, saying he wanted to make sure she knew what she was getting into. Finally, reluctantly, Damek left.

Ranger locked the door behind him, refreshed his drink, and sat in the living room. His erection had died, a victim of his conflicting emotions. From a purely analytical standpoint, the work he'd done on Shana had been a success. Not only had he introduced her to violent sex and bondage, but although she might not yet know it, he'd given her undeniable proof of why her friend was doing what she was. He'd been out of the *business* for several years but hadn't lost his touch. He still knew how to reach women and reduce them to what he needed them to be.

What he couldn't rid himself of was his self-loathing.

As a randy eighteen-year-old, he'd thought he had the world's greatest job. What young buck doesn't dream of working with naked, sexually stimulated females? He'd partaken of what was freely given countless times, and as a result, the women had blurred together in his mind — become breasts and bellies and cunts and little else.

Then he'd grown up. Seen past the fantasy behind Scarlet Cavern's walls to its underbelly. The moment of true awakening had taken place when he held a dead woman in his arms and known his father had been responsible.

So he'd turned his back on his heritage and forged a new career for himself and refused to acknowledge dark dreams during which he lost himself in breasts and bellies and cunts.

At least he had until Shana walked into his life.

She was successful, rich in her own right, talented and educated, to say nothing of beautiful. Unlike most of the beautiful women he'd come in contact with, she respected her brain more than she did her looks. Instead of being self-absorbed, she put friendship ahead of herself. How could he not admire her for that?

More than admire.

Love?

Lulled by drink and conflicting emotions, he dozed. Afternoon's shadows were creeping into the room when he woke. After a momentary disorientation, he realized he was hearing the sound of running water. What was it he'd been thinking about just before he fell asleep?

Feeling as if he'd just been shot, he acknowledged that for the first time in his life he'd thought of a woman in terms of love.

* * * * *

When the bathroom door opened, Shana turned toward the sound. She held a large soapy washcloth but made no attempt to cover her nakedness. It could be Damek, she told herself — Damek here to make good on his erection.

Then her nerve endings told her different. Ranger stood a few feet from the shower, arms folded over his chest, stance wide. She couldn't tell anything about his emotions.

"You're all right?" he asked.

"Tired. Sore. But all right. Where's Damek?"

"Gone."

Gone. Just the two of them. "He approves of what he saw? He'll let me in?"

"Yes."

Good. Maybe. "What happens now?" she asked as she went back to soaping her breasts.

"I told him we'd be there in three days."

"Because I need more — training?"

"No."

No. "Oh," she said but couldn't think of anything else. Her nipples looked red and were so sensitive they barely tolerated the washcloth. Gathering her courage, she moved the cloth to between her legs. Yes, she was tender there but not so much that she was immune to a touch to her clit.

"Join me, please," she begged.

He said nothing but removed his shoes. Next came his shirt and jeans and finally his shorts. Trembling, she moved to the side of the shower. When he stepped in, his eyes held on her face. He stood under the spray then ran his hands over her arms. His touch was gentle and felt like caring. Scared and excited, she waited for him to speak, but he only looked down at her. His dark eyes pulled her into him.

"I acted like a bitch in heat," she admitted. "Like I wanted to be mounted."

"Yes."

"Do—does it disgust you?"

"No. Does it you?"

"I don't know." She took his hands and joined him under the spray. "No, that's not an answer. When I woke up, everything came flooding back—the way I acted, the sounds I made."

She'd draped the washcloth over the control knobs. He picked it up, added more soap, and turned her so he could wash her back. After everything of hers he'd taken without asking permission, she longed to believe it was different this time.

"Is that why you took a shower?" he asked. "So you could clean off the memory?"

Even if I wanted to, I wouldn't be able to. "No. I—all right, I smelled like a racehorse."

"You don't anymore."

He'd started at her shoulders then moved down her spine. Now he reached her hips, and she wanted him to go on doing this forever. She'd thought the machine he'd used on her had wrung every bit of moisture out of her pussy, but she'd been wrong. She still had more to give— him?

"I don't want to talk about what happened," she said. "It's reality. I can't change anything."

"All right." He slid the cloth between her legs, and she spread them to increase his access. Water ran over her flesh, over both of them.

"Where do you live?" she asked.

"What do you care?"

"Ranger, please, what's been going on between us is intense. You can't pretend it isn't, can you?"

"No," he whispered. "I can't. All right, I bought a couple of acres that back up to Sweetwater Regional Park and built a log cabin in the middle."

"You built—"

He chuckled, and she embraced the lighthearted sound like a lifeline. "It was a kit. All I had to do was follow directions."

"Why such an isolated place?"

He said nothing for so long she wondered if she'd tried to venture someplace he had no intention of letting her go. *You have so many layers, so much complexity. You'll always fascinate me.*

"I had a lot of thinking to do—reassessing my life," he told her. "Deciding what I wanted to do with the rest of it." He turned her toward him and soaped her breasts. She wanted to help but lacked the strength to lift her arms. "By the time I'd finished the place and my bruises, blisters, and cuts had healed, I knew."

"That's when you went to work for Recovery?"

"Yeah." He stopped and stepped back so he could regard her. Once again his gaze pulled her into his depths. "I know what the underbelly looks like. Some people want it. If so, more power to them. I'm in no position to judge. But some, like me, want out. Need out."

He hadn't acted as if he wanted nothing to do with what Scarlet Cavern represented while he was *teaching* her the ropes. Unless she'd read him wrong—and she didn't believe she had—he'd enjoyed binding and chaining her as much as she'd loved being confined. Was that the only connection between them—a love of the dark side as he called it?

No! I won't believe that. I can't.

Belatedly she realized he was studying her, all of her. Just like that, her questions and thoughts evaporated. She cared about only one thing.

"Are you hungry?" he asked.

"Yes." Food had nothing to do with it.

* * * * *

After toweling herself and drying her hair under Ranger's watchful eye, Shana wrapped a large towel around herself and followed him into the kitchen. He'd dressed but of course, she had nothing. They passed by the living room on their way, but although she glanced at the front door, she had no wish to see if it was unlocked.

They collaborated on a salad and steak and ate sitting at the counter. She told him a little about what she did for a living, and he explained that he worked contract by contract and could pick and choose his assignments. He tried not to work during spring and summer.

"I never used to be that aware of the seasons," he explained. "But once I stopped spending my life indoors, I discovered nature. I love to hike and camp out. I've started mountain climbing and I'm a member of an endurance mountain biking team. Next year we're going to cover a portion of the Lewis and Clark trail."

She longed to go with him, to connect with this country's history, to spend long days and even longer nights in his company. For the first time in more than a month, her goal shifted. Lindsay's safety no longer consumed her.

But it should! It had to. "When we go there, what will happen?"

"You're ready to hear this?"

No! Gathering her courage and unexpected trust in Ranger, she said yes.

"What we've been doing—what I've been doing to you..."

"What?" Concentrating was easier if she didn't look at him so she busied herself cleaning up the kitchen.

"Only select people are allowed into the Cavern," he said. She could tell he was watching her every move. "I'll always have access, but even I can only bring certain people with me."

"How-how will you explain me?" she asked although she already believed she understood.

"They'll believe I've prescreened you and determined you're ready for the lifestyle. You'll be allowed in—on a probationary basis."

Her hands shook, forcing her clench them. "For what?"

"Shana, models like Lindsay are well-paid. They earn every penny."

"Because-because they're abused?" She felt sick.

"It looks like it to outsiders, to the tens of thousands who subscribe to the website, but it's part of the fantasy."

"I don't understand."

"Don't you?" he challenged. He stood and walked around to her side of the counter. Taking her hands, he flattened them against his chest. "Despite what you've gone through and the things you've learned about yourself, you still can't believe Lindsay wants the bondage life, can you?"

"No! I can't." She tried to pull free. "I—it's different for me because I'm motivated to-to help her."

"Let me ask you something. If your friend wasn't in the Cavern, you'd have no interest in going there, would you?"

How she wanted to lie and yell no, but Ranger knew things about her no one else ever had; he'd awakened a side of her she hadn't been aware of—or maybe hadn't had the opportunity to explore.

"Shana," he said. "There's something I don't understand. Maybe it shouldn't matter to me, but it does. Lindsay is your friend. You feel sorry for her because of her upbringing and the two of you share something because you were raped by the same man, but after all these years, you've stayed close."

"Yes."

"Why?"

He deserved a complete answer, and she wanted to give it to him. "Lindsay is the only person I've ever been totally honest with. I trust her. Do you understand, I trust her?"

"I'm trying to."

But it's hard because you've never had a relationship like that. "My parents didn't want me to model. The whole thing worried them; they were afraid I'd be exploited or discover it was so competitive I'd have my heart broken. I could have gotten a science scholarship, but I turned it down to pursue modeling."

"That pissed them off."

"Not pissed," she corrected. "My parents aren't like that. They've always been supportive, but they didn't understand what drove me. Lindsay did. She listened. She encouraged. She went with me to the early assignments and teased to keep me from being so scared. Then after several years modeling stopped being exciting for me, and she didn't want to housesit anymore. We took classes on running our own businesses, encouraged each other to stop dreaming and do something. I started designing clothes and shoes for girls in high school and college track, and she opened her pond construction company. We each became so busy; we didn't see each other as much as we used to. When I realized how long it had been, I tried to get in touch with her, but she didn't answer my messages. Then I..."

"Then one time when you were exploring a fantasy, you found her indulging in her own."

"I'm still not convinced that's what it is for her. Ranger, don't forget a woman died there. I have to know she's all right."

He nodded. "So do I."

"What? Are you saying you're doing this not just because you work for Recovery but because you want to make sure my friend is safe?"

"You've made her real to me. I need to be sure she's all right."

He cared about Lindsay! "Thank you for saying that," she admitted. "It means a great deal to me. What-what's going to happen when I get there?" she managed.

"You'll be tested."

Her legs threatened to buckle. "What?"

"It's the only way I can get you in. The Cavern skates a thin line which puts them at the edge of the law. If the management thought you were anything but a sub, they'd kick you out."

"You-you'll be there? You won't leave me, will you?"

"No, I won't."

Chapter Eleven

Shana wasn't sure how she'd gotten back in the living room. Ranger had said he needed to make some calls, and she might want to watch TV while she waited. After re-securing her towel, she turned on the TV but couldn't concentrate.

How naïve are you? She couldn't believe she hadn't wanted to know under what circumstances she'd be allowed in the Cavern. She'd been hiding her head in the sand, going one step at a time, focusing on the goal, not looking at the whole picture.

Well, now she had to.

What would be expected of her once the Cavern doors locked behind her? More of what she'd experienced at Ranger's hands?

Duh. What do you think?

"You can do it," she muttered. "No matter what it takes, as long as you find Lindsay, you'll do it."

With a shock she realized she no longer thought simply in terms of rescuing her friend. Could Lindsay really want what was happening to her?

No! Impossible!

But you like being controlled and sexually stimulated and rendered helpless.

Only because I trust Ranger.

Why, the devil's advocate demanded. *Why the hell do*

you trust him?

I don't know, she retorted. *I don't know!*

Should you trust?

What do you want? Everything tied up in a neat bow? Life isn't like that, all right. I've gotten to know him, better than I did at first at least. He's a complex human being, compassionate — I believe. He wanted to know how I feel about Lindsay; I know he did. He builds log cabins and goes for long hikes. He isn't afraid of hard work or sleeping under the stars.

And he can turn you inside out with a touch. Don't forget that. The man understands your body better than you do.

What are you saying?

Open your eyes. Don't let your body — and heart blind you.

The argument raged, making her slow to realize she was no longer alone. The room was filled with shadow, silent because she hadn't bothered to turn up the sound on the TV.

"Thursday," he said.

She swallowed against the tide of panic. "All right. I — what day is it?"

"Tuesday."

"Only two days."

"Slight change of plans. Manipulation on Damek's part. He's hot to see you again."

She'd curled up on the couch with her legs tucked under her. The towel was large enough to cover her thighs, but she couldn't dismiss how little effort it would take to render her naked again.

"What-what do we do in the meantime?"

"I'll keep you occupied. Ready."

She thought he'd sit down, but he continued to stand.

She couldn't dismiss his size or the way his stance drew her attention to what waited between his legs. They'd had sex once; she knew what kind of lover he was; no unknown remained.

Or did it?

"I want…" she started then faltered.

"What?" He stepped closer.

"I feel—I've felt nonstop sexually stimulated since I got here."

"You want to go back into the training room?"

"No," she whispered and stood up.

This close to him, she couldn't possibly misread his expression. Maybe she should have been prepared for his reluctance, the brief glimpse of a trapped animal. But she needed him to want her as much as she did him, the emotion clean and simple.

"Do you want me to beg?" she asked. "I know. It isn't—this isn't what our contract calls for. But we—"

"We've already fucked once so why not again?"

Hold me. I feel so alone. "Is that the way you want to put it?"

"It's the truth."

But fucking sounds so primal and primitive—bodies but nothing else joining. "Yes it is," she added, surprised by how detached she sounded. "If you said you wanted to wire my pussy again, I wouldn't stop you. I'd love the feeling. But—" Gathering her courage and need, she reached for his jeans' fastening. "I'm more than that part of my body, Ranger. I'm also a head, a heart."

Looking tense, he watched as she unzipped his jeans. Then she crouched and pulled them down. He hadn't put on shoes after tending to her in the shower and after a moment lifted his feet so she could remove the denim. She straightened slowly, hands on his flesh. His cock had already been partly erect, and her caress finished the job.

We shouldn't be doing this, his eyes said. *We don't want to cross this line.*

But she did. And so, she believed, did he.

She reached for the towel she'd fastened under her breasts, but he pulled her hands off her and positioned them behind her back. When he released them, she kept them there and looked up at him, breasts straining and hungry for his touch. He didn't rush the disrobing but slowly drew the towel off her. She felt like a gift to him, a hot and willing gift.

Not speaking because she had no words in her, she assisted in pulling his shirt over his head. Then she brought it to her face and breathed in his scent. After rubbing the shirt against her cheek, she dropped it on the carpet on top of her towel. He dispensed with his shorts.

Electrical current touched her fingertips. She hoped his flesh against hers would calm the vibration, but when she ran her hands over his belly, they became even more sensitive. He'd done so much for her, gifted her in so many ways. Her debt to him loomed over her, and she handled it in the only way she could think of.

Dropping to her knees before the man who'd countless times owned and stimulated her body, she took hold of his cock and again guided it into her mouth. She tasted the tip, ran her tongue along the slit and tasted a drop of cum. Working her muscles, she pulled in more of him. She felt his hands in her hair, dropped her haunches so she could look up and hold onto him at the same time.

His gaze spoke of caution and trust—and excitement. At the moment she loved him as she'd never loved before.

This powerful man was vulnerable. She held his most precious possession.

But he was more than just an erect cock.

I won't hurt you, she told him. *I'd never hurt you – any more than you've hurt me.*

She fondled his balls and drew in yet more of him. Her cunt muscles clenched. They remained tight and almost painful, prompting her to release him. When he pulled on her hair, compelling her to look up at him, again she smiled what she hoped was a reassuring smile before taking hold of his cock and resting it in the palm of her hand so she could stroke him with her tongue.

His engorged veins there fascinated her; she couldn't imagine ever growing tired of the exploration. He began kneading her temples, and she wondered if her veins might explode. She could suck him until he came and know she'd given him a gift, but today she didn't want to swallow his cum. She needed it…

Perhaps coming to the same conclusion, he pulled her to her feet. Then he guided her onto the couch and spread her legs. He placed her heels on the edge of the couch, knees bent, crotch open and waiting. Eager for the joining, she scooted forward and tried to lift her buttocks. She longed to reach for him, but her perch was too precarious.

He paused, his features shadowed and eyes dark with something she didn't want to explore. Gentle when she knew of what else he was capable of, he crouched and effortlessly slid into her. Her wet and swollen opening cradled him as if he'd long been lost from her. Despite the heat nipping at her nerves, for a breathless moment she thought of nothing except bringing him home.

Then he dropped to his knees and eased her toward him at the same time, their union still intact. After a little manipulation, she lay on her back with her feet on the floor, hands free to caress his forearms. Although she occasionally brought his face into focus, her attention remained on the wondrous feel of him inside her. His powerful thighs responded, allowing him to pump repeatedly into her.

"Not quite..." he started. He placed his hands under her hips and lifted her. From waist to knees she lost the distinction between the two of them. Because she'd flooded herself with her own juices, his cock glided in the home she'd provided. Still, she felt slight friction and warmed herself on it. She tried to match his movements, and although she felt the strain in her back, she kept herself arched for him.

What had been done to her lately had left her humming with sexual frustration, but degree by degree, thrust by thrust, he erased the emotion and gifted her with joy. She became a machine, a hot and eager machine, absorbed him, maybe became him.

The volcano took over, grabbed her sex and shook her with its power. Beyond control, she sobbed out her climax. He came at nearly the same time, driving his cock so deep in her it consumed her.

Spent and sweating, she slid off the couch and joined him on the floor. They lay belly to belly, bodies still joined, kissing eyelids, cheeks, lips.

Chapter Twelve

"I lied," Ranger said. "You aren't ready."

Shana scrambled to her feet and stared at her sex partner, her lover, her what? When she'd finally regained her senses after they'd fucked in the living room, Ranger had guided her back to what she now considered *her* bedroom and told her to get some rest. She'd tried to entice him to join her, but he'd said he had things he had to do. Although she'd wanted to think about him — about them — exhaustion had pulled her down.

Now she stood naked in front of the again clothed Ranger. Because the room lacked windows, she didn't know how much time had passed since she'd fallen asleep or whether it was night or day. "Aren't ready for what?" she managed to ask.

"To enter the Cavern." Instead of demanding an answer she suspected she wouldn't get anyway, she resigned herself to waiting for his next move. Images of his tenderness and passion flitted through her mind, but those memories were at odds with what she now saw. He'd dressed all in black and held what she assumed was yet another gag. This one consisted of two leather straps held together by an equal number of metal rings. He stepped toward her.

"You're satisfied, aren't you?" His question held no tenderness. "A woman well-fucked."

"Yes."

"But if you went to the Cavern like that, you'd never be able to pull it off so it's my job to take you back to what you were before."

"Your job?" Her legs suddenly felt weak.

"What you hired me for, remember. We have a contract." He took another step and held up the gag so she could better see it. He demonstrated how to twist one of the rings slightly, breaking the circle and allowing him to free one of the leather strips. "Take it," he ordered.

Feeling as if she'd never seen this man before, she did so but held it by her fingertips.

"Put one of the leather pieces in your mouth and loop the other behind your head so the rings are near your cheeks. Do it, now!"

She jumped at the sharp order. Although she couldn't get her hands to stop trembling, she managed to follow his directions. Not satisfied with her compliance, he ordered her to again slip the leather into the metal and snap the ring closed. Begging *no* with her eyes, she completed her task. The gag felt snug and rendered her incapable of making more than garbled sounds.

"Why did you silence yourself, Shana?" he asked. "Because you're afraid of me or because you're eager for what other things I have up my sleeve?"

I don't know. Both maybe.

"I could continue to explain why we're having this lesson," he said as he checked the gag. "But I don't like repeating myself. Besides, I want you keyed into your responses, not listening to me talk. Soon I'll take over, but for a little while I want you part of the process."

He grabbed her hair and pulled her head back. Alarmed, she clamped her fingers around his wrists.

"No!" he ordered. "Hands off me. The only time you touch me is when I give you permission, and it isn't going to happen now."

Although she struggled to do as he commanded, when he increased his grip on her hair, instinct took over. Her nails pressed into his flesh.

"No!" he repeated. Releasing her hair, he quickly rotated his wrists and freed himself. Before she could think what to do, he twisted her arms behind her. Just like that, she felt her pussy heat. Was there no distinction between fear and arousal?

He used his hold to propel her toward the dresser. "I'm going to let you go," he said. "When I do, you're going to stand here and listen to my order. When you understand, you'll nod your comprehension. Then you'll complete your task."

What game are you playing? What happened to you?

She was still formulating the questions when he released her. Her arms dropped to her side. She couldn't bring herself to look at him. How long had it been since she'd worn anything? How long since she'd felt like a modern and in-command woman?

"You're going to open the drawer," he explained. "Pull out four lengths of white cotton rope. You'll give three to me and fold the remaining one in half. Then you'll take the twin strands and loop them twice around your waist. I'd let you tie them, but I want them done a certain way. Don't worry about the other three pieces right now. You'll understand their purpose as we proceed. Do you have that?"

Rendered mute by her own doing, she nodded.

"Good. Remember this, Shana. There are times to fight

and times to submit. Today is about submitting and experiencing the accompanying pleasures. Get started."

Her 4-H cattle had dutifully followed her into the show pen where they'd been bid on and bought so they could be slaughtered. As she opened the drawer and closed her now numb fingers over the ropes, she remembered how she'd felt like a Judas for leading the faithful animals to their death.

Sick and yet undeniably anticipating, she handed all but one rope to Ranger. She wrapped the strands around her waist and held onto the ends.

"Good job." His smile didn't extend beyond his mouth. He took the ends from her, ordered her to put her hands down at her sides, and snugged the rope belt in place before deftly tying it. It wasn't tight enough to be uncomfortable, and the soft cotton didn't irritate her skin. He looped another rope under the waist constraint in front so he had two equal lengths.

"Hands up," he ordered. "At your waist, fingers laced together."

What are you going – ?

"Now!"

She jumped and struggled to remember how he wanted her fingers positioned. As he began wrapping her wrists with the rope attached to her waist restraint, she struggled against the growing heat between her legs. The gag had been the first step in this latest imprisonment. What she'd put around her waist hadn't seemed that important but now-now she could no longer use her hands. Ranger's control had increased.

When he was finished, he stepped back and nodded at what she surmised was designed to give her permission to test what he'd done. The wrist restraints didn't cut off her circulation, but neither could she separate her hands or move them more than an inch in any direction. The knots were positioned so she couldn't reach them with her fingers.

"Inch by inch. Freedom by freedom," he said. "I don't know if you've noticed, but it's a beautiful day. A day to be outside. Let's go."

Leaving her by the drawer, he walked over to the door and opened it. "Good job, Shana. You know not to move until you're given permission."

Permission. I've never...

"Follow me," he ordered.

* * * * *

She hadn't been curious about the backyard before and should have been, Shana acknowledged when she stood next to Ranger under a massive oak tree with low spreading branches. The ground was soft from years and layers of leaves, the breeze a gentle murmur.

"A beautiful day." He pushed her hair back from her cheeks with an almost tender gesture. "A day to spend outdoors. I missed so many opportunities to be out in the fresh air when I was young. Tell me, do you enjoy being under the sun? Oh, that's right. You can no longer talk."

His words were heavy with meaning, but she couldn't quite grasp their essence. Despite herself, she contemplated her chances of running. Having her arms close to her body restricted her ability to run full out, and the gag made pulling in adequate air all but impossible. Besides, how could she explain to anyone what she was doing naked and bound like this?

Belatedly, she realized Ranger had thrown a rope over an overhead branch and was bringing the ends into alignment. Mesmerized, she watched.

"I don't want you going anywhere I don't intend you to," he explained in a voice devoid of emotion. "Controlling a sub's movements means a great deal to both the dom and the sub. Come closer. Stand next to me."

What are you — ? What are we — ?

The questions were still taking form inside her when he roughly grabbed her wrist restraints and hauled her against him. Once he'd positioned her below the branch rope, he ran a hand over her belly and between her legs. Confused and excited, she increased her stance.

"Ready for the next step, are you?" His words seemed to caress her skin. "Eager for today's lesson, or should I say the continuation?"

The leather in her mouth was wet, but that was nothing compared to the moisture she felt in her pussy, moisture he could effortlessly access.

"Your body has turned against you, Shana. It does what it wants to, what it needs to. Listen to the message." He stroked her drenched labia. "Surrender to it."

I have. I have no choice.

Leaving her cunt, he gripped her hips and positioned her so her body faced his. Then he returned to her crotch and pressed against her inner thighs, the pressure letting her know he expected her to separate her legs even more. On fire, she obeyed.

She didn't know what to think when he slipped the rope between her legs, stepped behind her, and pulled it up so it lay between her ass cheeks and over her anus. Scared, she stumbled back.

"No! Not going to happen." He punctuated his command by looping an arm over her hips and pulling her against him. At the same time, he worked the ass rope under the one circling her waist and cinched it tight. Her attention immediately shifted to the pressure on her labial lips, forcing her to try to look down at herself. She was still struggling to make sense of what he had in mind when he yanked on the ass rope and secured it to the cotton belt.

Barely comprehending, Shana stood on tiptoe and struggled to assess what had happened. He'd roped her to the tree, caught her to it much as she'd once tethered a calf to a fence. Only instead of using a halter, he'd brought her in line via the cotton strands between her legs and secured to her waist.

Mewling low in her throat, she took a tentative step. The rope against her crotch tightened, and she stopped.

"You're one with the tree," Ranger said. "Until I've decided you've had enough, you're going to stand here and take it."

The strands against her labia bit into sensitive flesh, prompting her to slide forward, but he'd tied her securely. There was no give, no freedom, no relief. Trembling in every cell, she fought to bring Ranger into focus.

He'd put distance between them once he'd secured the crotch rope, but now he closed in on her again. "I could use a spreader bar," he said. "Force you to stand with your legs apart, but I don't think it's going to be necessary. What does it feel like, Shana? As if you're tied by your pussy? You can't cry or beg, can't even curse me. And every time you shift position, the rope's going to rub against your clit."

Her clit!

"I use the softest cotton available," he explained. "Some doms swear by nylon, but cotton is absorbent, and you're getting wet, aren't you?"

She'd been so focused on what he was doing to her, she'd briefly forgotten about her reaction. Damn it, he was right! The crotch rope pressed relentlessly, exciting already sensitive flesh and forcing a response.

Torn between hating him and gratitude for this latest chapter in her sexual education, she struggled to not jump when he slid his hand between her legs. The way he fingered her labial lips so they were positioned on either side of the rope, his practiced tug on the taut strands left no doubt of his conviction that he owned her.

He did! He'd taken her so far, introduced her to so much! No matter how unnerving, she'd follow him into the sexual depth!

"It wouldn't take much, would it?" he observed as he stroked her ass. "The slightest bit more stimulation and you'd be off." He wrapped an arm around her hip and pulled her off-balance toward him. The rope's grip on her sex increased, blurring the line between pain and pleasure. Lowering his head, he sucked a nipple into his mouth. She sobbed into the gag; no matter how much she tried, she couldn't remain still. If only she could increase the friction/pressure against her clit! Just a little more and she'd...

"No!" he commanded and released her. "Not going to happen."

* * * * *

You're an asshole! Born one and going to die one.

Despite a wave of self-disgust and hatred he couldn't

remember ever feeling before, Ranger forced himself to compartmentalize his emotions, shelve them away until he dared examine them in detail. What he lacked the ability — the strength — to do was disassociating himself from the helpless creature staring at him. He'd debated binding her hands behind her, but she was more comfortable this way, and although the subject's comfort shouldn't be his concern, it was.

He'd gone back into the house for a trio of whips. In the past he would have left the subject alone for an hour or so to contemplate the pressure against her pussy and more fully comprehend her dependence on him, he hadn't been able to bring himself to do that to Shana. Besides, he wanted to be near her even if she hated him.

"You have a choice." He held up the three whips and shook them so she could see their silken strands. "Technically there isn't much difference between them. Mostly cosmetic. This one," he indicated the longest, "looks impressive, but the strands are so limp there's hardly any snap to it. Most of the women I've worked with prefer the short ones. They say it feels like an electrical charge. Then there's the in-between size which is actually the easiest for me to control, not that I suspect you're concerned with that. Which is it going to be?"

She continued to gaze into his eyes. Her stare spoke of sexual heat, discomfort and excitement. Most of all her look said she trusted him.

Trust? This incredible woman trusted him?

"You want me to make the decision?" he made himself ask. When she nodded and the corners of her mouth twitched, he wondered which of them held the upper hand. Not at all sure where this would end, he selected the medium length and dropped the others to the ground. "Is there anything you're afraid to tackle?" he asked.

She shrugged, reminding him that he'd taken away her ability to speak. The need to communicate with her nearly overwhelmed him, but it was safer this way. Distance, maybe, would keep him on task—and sane.

"You're pretty cocky, aren't you?" he continued. "I'm sure you believe I'm as turned on as you are."

She dropped her gaze to his all but screaming cock then tilted her head to the side. Her eyes danced with laugher.

"You're wrong, damn you. I'm the one getting you ready for what you're so all-fired determined to accomplish. We do it my way."

Her laughter didn't die, but it faded a bit. She shifted position, her features contorting. No wonder. She'd been forced onto her toes, and he could only guess what the rope was doing to her trapped pussy. The line between pain and pleasure had been crossed. Until he returned her to pleasure, he couldn't keep her hungry.

Stepping behind her, he loosened the knots holding the crotch rope taut. Although she remained tethered to the branch, she now stood flat-footed with the rope barely brushing her reddened labia.

"Spread your legs," he commanded.

She sighed but did as he ordered. Unless he was mistaken—which he didn't believe he was—her juices had drenched the cotton. Determined to answer what had become an important question, he ran his fingers over her crotch. She straightened, her thigh muscles tightened.

"Still wet, wetter than earlier in fact," he said. "Not that I need to tell you. The matter under debate," he stroked her again, "is whether you can come from something as simple as a rope."

Her attention held on what she could see of his hand. He suspected her own bound hands kept her from having a clear view. In addition, they both knew she wasn't going anywhere.

"Disconcerting, isn't it? You can't do anything except stand there and take whatever I dish out. And if you displease me in any way," he stroked an inner thigh with the whip, "like kicking me or even trying to, I'll leave you here until I'm good and ready." The whip trailed over the other thigh. "Puts the burden on you, Shana. Unless you want to spend the rest of the day like this — and maybe the night too — you're going to do what I want. Aren't you?" He punctuated the question by slapping her labia with the flat of his hand.

She flinched and took what he had no doubt was an involuntary step back. The harness stopped her. He slapped her again, relishing in her wet heat. Damn but she was hot! A woman any man would want.

But she wasn't his. They had a business relationship and nothing more.

I'm so sorry it's this way, he mentally told her. *If we'd met under any other conditions, things might be different for us — good.*

But he came from darkness while she represented what was good about life.

Feeling as if he'd been punched, he fought emotion and reverted back to what he'd once been. "Your best shot at winning the trust of those at the Cavern is by being the ultimate in what they want in a woman," he said. He'd placed a few inches of distance between her crotch and his hand while talking, but enough was enough! Even if he wound up as sexually frustrated as she was, he couldn't keep his hands off her. All too soon their reason for being together would end, and he'd never see her again. This was all he had. Every moment counted; the memories would have to last for the rest of his life.

"And what they want," he worked his thumb under the rope and rubbed his flesh against her clit, "is a woman ready and able to put on a show. And a woman who's been teased but not satisfied puts on one hell of a show."

He looked at her and wasn't surprised to see she was no longer smiling, no longer looking as if she had any control over herself.

"Legs wider," he ordered. "Make yourself as open as possible."

Shuffling awkwardly, she fully exposed herself. His cock shuddered, his head pounded. It would take so little—nothing really—to strip himself naked and give them both what they desperately needed.

But he couldn't. He didn't dare because his heart might not survive.

Teeth grinding and legs all but numb, he walked behind her, reached around her and closed his arm over her collarbone. He pulled her toward him, but when she tried to adjust her stance so she could keep her balance, he slapped her belly with the whip.

"Did I give you permission to move? Did I?"

Whimpering, she shook her head.

Keeping pressure on her with his arm, he began tattooing her mons with the whip. The blows—if they could be called that—made a whispering sound.

He lost himself in the murmur of flesh and silken

strands, felt his own muscles melt into hers. She gave up trying to retain her balance and leaned against his chest. He felt her legs tremble and imagined the strain in her well-muscled thighs and calves. Most of all he thought about her soft and vulnerable pussy and the unrelenting arousal he was inflicting on her. Her hands hampered his aim, but he improvised by sliding her slightly to the side.

His arm pistoned up and down, up and down, treating and teasing, teaching her the meaning of endless, learning the full meaning of involvement. The whip became an extension of himself, not his cock of course, but in essence flesh against flesh. She broke out in sweat. It soaked through his shirt and dampened him, met with his own heat.

And because he'd been trained in the ways of a woman's body, he intuitively kept tabs on her progress. Her climax was coming, building, stalled because of her awkward position, but not dying. Hardly. Instead, he kept her on the brink — kept them both there.

For what felt like forever.

Chapter Thirteen

Shana couldn't stop shaking. Maybe she wouldn't feel so nervous if Ranger had told her more about what to expect, but he'd barely said a word to her today beyond showing her what he'd chosen for her to wear.

She shouldn't be surprised by the outfit, she chided as she stared at herself in the mirror. The black bra pushed her breasts up and out in ways she didn't know breasts could go, and she didn't want to think about how he'd made his selection. She had on black sheer nylons held in place with a blood-red garter belt. He hadn't supplied her with panties. Her heels were painfully high, forcing her to admit she couldn't so much as take a normal step in them. The blouse was white silk and lace, a fanciful concoction that would have made her feel like a princess if it hadn't been so transparent. And the black leather skirt—the damn thing barely covered her ass.

"I look like a hooker," she informed her image. "Well-heeled but a hooker just the same."

"Come on out," Ranger called. She tried to read something in his tone but couldn't.

Stepping out, she spotted him standing by the front door. He held a short length of leather. "What's going to happen when we get there?" she blurted although she'd just told herself not to ask. "You'll be with me all the time, won't you?"

"Yeah. You're my possession."

"Your what?" If she hadn't been afraid she'd lose her footing, she'd have bolted back into the room she both loved and hated.

"It's part of the fantasy, Shana. The *slaves* buy into it as completely as the *masters* do."

Not this broad. I'm no one's possession.

But maybe she was. After all, hadn't she turned her body and nearly her soul over to him? In the past two days, she'd worn ropes and chains, tasted leather and more gag balls, had her legs both spread-eagled and lashed together.

Ranger had taken a video of her riding a sawhorse which cut into her pussy and made her lie on the floor while he immobilized her with plastic wrap. By the end of each session, she'd been so turned on she thought she'd lose her mind and had been hot to jump his bones, but he'd refused to have sex with her. Not once had he allowed her to climax.

"You're going to be tested," was all he'd said when she'd begged for release. "It'll be easier if you're horny. You'll come quickly."

"Quickly?" she'd shot at him. "I'm a time bomb set to go off."

"Which means I've done my job."

His job? Surely it had been more than that for him. It had to be.

"You understand the rules, don't you?" he asked now. "As soon as you're on camera, you need to act like a reluctant captive. Out and out fighting restraints isn't necessary, but at the beginning you don't want to give the impression you're enjoying yourself."

"Restraints?"

"Nothing more than we've already worked with. This is your last chance. Either we go now, or you tell me you want to drop the whole thing."

"You know I can't do that. I'm too close to Lindsay to quit now."

"And if you learn you've gone through all this for nothing, and she's happy doing what she is?"

"I'll never know unless I talk to her," she snapped. *And I have to see what goes on in that place. After all this build-up, I must experience what it has to offer.* Determined to appear more confident than she felt, she indicated what was in his hand. "The rest of my costume?"

"Your collar," he said.

Not a necklace, a collar. "Oh," she managed.

As if sensing her turmoil, he walked over and brushed her hair off her throat. He briefly showed her the slender dark leather with a metal loop riveted into it then fastened the collar around her neck. Although it wasn't tight enough to restrict her breathing, she thought of it as a choker.

"Before the night is over," he said, "you might see Lindsay."

And once I have, what about you and me?

She couldn't bring herself to ask either of them the question. "I need to thank you," she said instead. "You've given all your time to me, put your own life on hold."

"You've done the same thing by putting your friend first."

But she isn't the only reason I'm doing this, not anymore. You—I'm changed in ways I couldn't anticipate. "I never asked. If I hadn't come to Recovery, what would you be doing?"

He scanned his surroundings then shrugged. "It doesn't matter."

Do I matter?

* * * * *

Because Lindsay had been photographed in what looked like a dungeon, Shana had no idea what to expect of the building known as Scarlet Cavern. To her shock, Ranger drove them to an exclusive community at the edge of the Pacific Ocean. Every one of the multimillion dollar mansions was surrounded by a security fence and situated on several treed acres affording privacy. They drove up to a locked gate. Ranger announced himself at a remote speaker, and the gate swung open. It closed behind them.

"Scared?" he asked.

"Do you blame me?" she asked although her heart raced with anticipation and excitement. "I'm not—they aren't going to hurt me, are they?"

"It depends on your pain threshold, something I have a pretty good handle on."

Less than encouraged by his explanation, she concentrated on taking in her surroundings. The main house had two levels, and she guessed the total square footage at over 5,000. The exterior was brick, and tile covered the roof. Several windows on the second story had bars on them, and the heavy wooden front door would have looked right on a castle. She half expected to see guards and Dobermans. Instead, when Ranger pulled into the circular drive, a burly young man came out and opened her door.

"Welcome," he said cordially. "We're expecting you. I

trust you had a pleasant drive. The ocean is spectacular. Unfortunately, you can't see it until you go to the back of the house."

"I'm looking forward to it," she said as she exited and perched on her impossible heels. In truth, the view had nearly been the last thing on her mind.

"Things aren't quite ready," the man told Ranger as the three of them walked toward the house. "We had another shoot earlier in the day. Things are still being put back together. Besides, I imagine the young lady would appreciate a tour first."

On the brink of thanking the man, it occurred to Shana that he'd been addressing Ranger, not her.

Ranger said that yes, becoming comfortable with the setting and some of the people she'd be working with was a priority.

They entered an enormous room filled with expensive, modern furniture with chrome and micro-fiber fabric most predominant. None of the chairs or couches looked particularly comfortable, making her wonder if people actually sat in here. The hardwood floor was highly polished, and she winced at the thought of what her heels might do to it. However, the muscular young man didn't seem to care.

"This is mostly for show," he explained, indicating the room. "We hired an interior decorator and this is what she came up with. Eventually we'll make some changes."

Beyond the living room, if that's what it was, she spotted a spacious dining room with a table large enough to serve maybe twenty people. Their guide dismissed it with a shrug and guided them toward another opening. A moment later Shana found herself in a dark room done in red velvet and rich drapes. The furniture had a Victorian feel, but mostly it put her in mind of Hollywood's idea of what a brothel looked like.

"We've made some modifications since you were here," the guide told Ranger. "I think you'll agree that much of the furniture is more functional."

With a shock, Shana realized that the couches and recliners came with an assortment of metal rings. Ropes were attached to some of them. In addition, more rings had been imbedded in the ceiling and walls. There were even several on the floor at the edge of the thick area rug. She longed to cling to Ranger, but he acted as if she didn't exist.

"Looks tacky," Ranger said.

The young man laughed. "That's the whole idea, isn't it? In truth, it isn't used that much since most people prefer the dungeons or outside. Outdoor work presents problems with lighting, but our customers seem to favor it so we try to accommodate them. Right now we're working on a serial story with five of the *slaves*. If there's time, I'll show you what we filmed yesterday. Things have changed a lot recently, for the better I dare say. The fantasy element has become more realistic."

Shana could barely believe what she was hearing. She glanced at Ranger to see if he was as shocked, but he showed no emotion.

"Your father's hand at the helm is missed, Ranger," the man said. "He had a way of keeping everyone on-task that was lost when decisions started being made by committee. I know you'd be welcomed back if —"

"It isn't going to happen, Sal."

For the first time, the young man's demeanor became

serious. "None of us understand—"

"I know you don't. It's enough that I do. Now, let's get started."

* * * * *

Despite her growing excitement, Shana nearly bolted when a man with tattooed forearms informed her that her session would take place on the beach. She didn't know what she'd expected—surely a contract to sign and some information about what they intended to do with her. Shouldn't she be able to okay or veto?

As if anticipating her questions, Sal explained that Ranger had already dealt with the legal technicalities. She'd be paid $500 for her work, and if her performance met with approval, future work and a raise would be forthcoming. Wondering if this is what it felt like to work for a temporary agency, she tried to wrap her mind around the idea of being subjected to whatever tattoo man decided to do with her.

Sal had led her and Ranger to a large redwood deck overlooking the ocean. A middle-aged man and a slightly younger skinny woman were already outside and seemed more interested in their camera equipment than her. Then tattoo man had returned with a pack slung over his shoulder. He plunked himself in a lounge chair and appraised her as if she was a piece of horseflesh.

"Great boobs. Are they real?"

"Yes," she retorted.

"Good. We've got customers who go off every time they see a model with plastic jobs." He chuckled. "Then there's an equal amount who want to see them, so go figure. What about the tan? Fake and bake?"

She glanced at Ranger who looked disinterested in the conversation. "Do you mean do I use a tanning booth? No. I don't trust them."

"Then we'll be showing a bikini line. Everyone likes those. Getting to the important stuff, what turns you on the most?"

"What?"

He leveled a *What are you, stupid?* look. "Bondage, pain, sensory deprivation, what gets you off?"

This time she couldn't have answered if he'd held a gun to her head. She was also glad no one knew what was going on between her legs. Damn it, the conversation was turning her on even more!

"Medium pain," Ranger supplied. "She's good with strong bondage, being handled when she can't do anything about it."

Tattoo man had the audacity to lick his lips. "My favorite pastime, nearly favorite anyway. I hope you haven't banged her lately. If you have, it'll make getting her to come harder."

"She's ripe," Ranger said. He slid his arm around her waist and pulled her toward him. She thought he'd grab her breasts or run his hands between her legs to demonstrate. Instead, he gave her a quick but tender squeeze and kissed her cheek. Instantly, she felt lightheaded and alive—in love.

How had that happened? Did he feel the same way?

"All right, Shana," tattoo man said. "As soon as the cameras are ready to go, we'll start. I'm a damn good rigger if I do say so myself. None of the women have complained about my rope work, but I've just finished with some iron modifications so that's what I'll be using.

Let me show you."

Looking like a proud parent, he opened his bag and hauled out heavy-duty ankle restraints, a thick but flexible metal loop she assumed would fit around her waist, and narrower metal fashioned in a figure eight.

Ranger pointed at the figure eight. "What's that?"

"Like it? Handcuffs. I'll fasten her arms behind her with one wrist over the other. Once I've hooked it to the waist restraint, she won't have any play in her arms. It pulls her shoulders back, accentuating the boobs." He held up clunky-looking ankle cuffs. "Like the chain? A little overkill for those delicate legs of yours but the customers get off on all that metal confining a sweet young body." He winked. "I've never had a complaint from the models either, especially those who put bondage at the top of their gotta have list."

Unable to admit she was becoming even more turned on, Shana told herself fear was making her wet. Only one thing was lacking—Ranger.

"We're going to play in the sand." He pointed at the shore. "Nothing like sand all over a sweet, tanned body to please the customers. I'd put on suntan lotion, but then the sand would really stick to you. Fortunately, it's late afternoon so you shouldn't get burned before the sun sets. Should be a great sunset. I want to capture as much of it as possible."

Despite her conflicting emotions, she had to admire tattoo man's dedication to his-his art. "How many people will see me?"

"The photographers of course. Ranger, I assume you'll stay on the set?"

Ranger nodded, and she barely stifled a sigh of relief.

At the same time, she wanted him to protest and say only he had any right to touch her.

"That's it then. The beach is private. The neighbors leave us alone."

Because they know what goes on? "Ah, when I went to the Internet site, I noticed that sometimes you had more than one-one woman in the shoot. I thought you might..."

Tattoo man grinned. "You saying you swing both ways? Maybe you want a little company?"

"No! I-I was just curious."

"This is new for her," Ranger supplied. "What about it, Shana? Do you want to talk to other models first?"

Tattoo man grunted impatiently, but she was grateful for Ranger's suggestion. She *had* to stay focused. Everything was about Lindsay.

"Is it possible?" she asked. "How many women are kept here?"

"Kept? Whatever gave you that idea? True, at any given time we have one or more woman on the premises, but that's because either they're involved in multiple shoots in a short timeframe or they're temporarily without housing elsewhere."

"What do you mean?"

For the first time, the man looked serious. "Some of our models aren't the most stable women around. They get hung up on the role-playing that goes on here and want to play into the fantasy that this is some kind of harem, thus the bars on a few windows. In fact—" He stared at Ranger, then looked back at her. "You wouldn't be here if Ranger hadn't vouched for your stability. There's a fine line between a healthy sexual appetite and a whacko-pain-slut. Those women need a shrink, not us."

That wasn't Lindsay. It couldn't be!

"Margaret, you ready?" tattoo man asked the woman photographer.

"No shit. We don't wanna lose the sun."

Shana's heart leaped into her throat. She gaped at Ranger who, to her relief, winked. *Thank you*, she told him with her eyes. *I couldn't do this without you.*

Not sure whether she was stalling or making an honest attempt to learn something about Lindsay, she spoke. "One of the teaser clips I saw showed you with a tall blonde who'd had what looked like string tied to her nipples. I don't see how you could get that to stay on."

He chuckled. "Lindsay. Talk about jugs! Trick of the trade. I got her nipples hard first with ice. Then the string went on easy. If you'd bought into the service, you'd have seen some close-ups of the marks I made. Lindsay's a real player, a great actress."

"Actress?"

"Yeah. The customers want realism."

He said something else but she couldn't concentrate. Lindsay was here, willingly? Was it true? How much longer before she'd see her and assure herself that her friend was all right?

"Speaking of which," tattoo man said. "I want you to play to the cameras and ignore them at the same time, if you know what I mean."

"I've done a lot of modeling but…"

"But you're not used to being distracted."

He must have sensed her confusion because he continued. "That's part of why you're here for this test. Ranger says you really get into the game, that your climaxes are real."

"He said—" Feeling betrayed somehow, she wanted to glare at Ranger but didn't dare look at him. "He told you...about me?"

"Everything I need to know. Look, we've got to get rolling. I'm going to want you to struggle and look as if you're being held against your will. Work your body, give us everything you've got, and you could make more money having fun than you could ever imagine."

This couldn't be real! She couldn't be following a stranger down the stairs to begin something designed to give who knows how many dirty old men a sexual thrill. But it was because she believed this was the only way she'd see Lindsay—and because despite her conflicting emotions, she wanted to experience *everything*.

Was this her or the woman Ranger had turned her into?

"Lose the shoes," tattoo man said. "They'll bog down in the sand. Okay, here's what I'm thinking. It'll look hokey, but I want you to be traipsing along the beach. You've found this deserted stretch and have decided to pull back your blouse so you can tan your boobies. I'll come along acting like I'm looking for seashells or some shit. Then I'll grab you from behind and throw you to the ground. Fight me but not really, you got it? I'll take it from there."

Chapter Fourteen

Knowing Ranger was on the deck was the only thing that kept Shana from bolting at first. He'd kissed her, a gentle, comforting peck! *How much do I matter to you? Please, please care as much as I do.*

As she sauntered along the beach, she tried to concentrate on the warm sand on her toes, and lowering sun in her eyes. She'd been before countless cameras; she could do this. When the male photographer positioned himself ahead of her, she stopped and faced the ocean. Smiling faintly, she unbuttoned her blouse and revealed the curve of her breasts. She threw herself into the scene by running her fingers over her breasts and parting her lips. In her mind, she became a sensual woman taking everything the warm afternoon had to offer.

Tattoo man was heading her way, his progress recorded by the other photographer. She pretended to notice him for the first time and debate whether to cover herself again. Shrugging, she turned her attention back to the sun. The man trudged past without looking at her. She'd actually started to relax when something hit her from behind and sent her to the ground.

"What the — ?" she started. The man straddled her and pressed against her buttocks. Her hands flailed, but she couldn't reach behind her to dislodge him. She tried kicking back. He waited until she'd stopped, then slid his hands between her legs.

"Look what I've got here," he said loud enough for

the camera to catch his words. "My own little sea nymph. What about it? Need some tanning, do you?"

She'd had to turn her head to the side to keep her mouth out of the sand. He stopped groping between her legs and hoisted the short skirt up around her waist. Out of the corner of her eye, she saw one of the cameras close in for a shot of her now exposed ass.

"What's this, bitch?" Her captor ran a finger between her ass cheeks. "Half-naked already. I knew you were asking for it. Oh, we're going to have fun today. At least I am. If I work you right, so will you."

She made what she hoped were sounds of distress, but although in real life she would have been screaming her head off, she didn't. *Ranger! She'd think of him, use him to hold onto her sanity.*

The man grabbed her right ankle and pulled her leg back toward him. Although she probably could have yanked loose, she didn't put her full strength into the effort. She came close to losing it when he fastened the heavy metal around her ankle and barely noticed when he cuffed her other ankle. The chain was no more than a foot long, severely restricting her movement.

"First step accomplished," he announced. "No matter what you try, you won't be running. So, let's take a look at you."

He climbed off her and hauled her to her feet. In the struggle, the blouse buttons had come undone. She started to cover herself, but he twisted her hand behind her back. When she tried to turn toward him, she stepped on the chain and nearly fell. Feeling like a roped horse, she struggled to remember this was playacting. With Ranger, excitement had lapped at her, but right now she felt nothing sexual.

"Oh yes, you're a prime one." He accented his declaration by pushing one bra cup down, exposing her breast. "Love the merchandise."

Not sure what he wanted from her, she resorted to whimpering and giving him a pleading look as he removed her blouse. He left the bra in place—kind of.

"Tell you what, bitch. I'm a sporting man so I'm going to give you one last chance to escape. Go on! Run!"

Taking that as her cue, she sprang forward. An instant later she lay in the sand again.

"Want to hang around, do you?" He dropped to his knees beside her and began rubbing the small of her back. She tried to get off her belly then surrendered when he pulled first one arm and then the other behind her. The figure eight manacle crossed her wrists one over the other, elbows sticking out. He'd left her with enough freedom— if it could be called that—to slide her arms up and down a few inches. *Where was the waist cinch he was so proud of?*

"Now we're making progress. You'll spend plenty of time in the sand, but first I'm going to check out the merchandise."

Once again he pulled her to her feet. Her hair had fallen forward, half blinding her, and sand had gotten into her bra and garter belt. Still, there was something about the sensation...

Demonstrating his skill at working to the camera, he slowly and deliberately fingered her body. He began by exposing her other breast then both pinched and suckled on them until her nipples ached. Next he turned his attention to her body below the waist, testing the elasticity in the garter belt, forcing her to spread her legs as far as the chain allowed so he could tug on her labia. Feeling disassociated from her body, she moaned and begged him not to hurt her.

Both camera people came closer. One scanned her body so intimately she felt as if she was being sucked into the lens. The other concentrated on tattoo man as he teased, probed, and prodded like some livestock judge. He turned her so her back was to the ocean and forced her to lean over. Once he had her in position, he spread her buttocks; she had no doubt the camera had zeroed in.

She wasn't turned on! She wasn't!

As if hearing her and wanting to point out her lie, her captor ran his fingers over her opening. "Getting wet there, are you, cunt? Don't worry. We're just getting started."

Seeking to separate herself to the spectacle she presented, she straightened as much as she could and stared up at the deck. Ranger stood with his hands gripping the railing, his expression unreadable.

I need you! Want you! Not this…

"You're looking mighty empty down here." Her captor's thumb entered her sex. "Need something to fill the hole. I'd like to personally fulfill that requirement, but if I do, I'll get so involved in what I'm doing I won't be able to play with you. One thing—" He slipped a hand under her garter belt in front. "You're way overdressed for what I have in mind."

To her surprise, the photographers stopped filming. The woman lit a cigarette. Tattoo man released her and pulled a key out of his back pocket. "Not bad," he said. "What do you think?" he asked the woman. "Not having trouble with shadows, are you?"

"Nah." She glanced up at the sun. "Get hopping though. It's countdown time."

Shana sighed in relief when the man uncuffed her wrists. She rubbed them while he freed her ankles. Just like that, her arousal faded, something she couldn't remember having experienced when Ranger handled her. "What's going to happen now?" she asked.

"Scene change. Get out of those clothes, and I'll hook you back into my contraption. Good job with the vocals, by the way. Sounded like you wanted nothing to do with me—and the way you're getting wet, great. Ranger knew what he was talking about when he vouched for your responsiveness."

That's why you drove me half-crazy, isn't it Ranger? So I'd be primed for this. But do I thank or curse you?

"Back off, Tat. I'm taking over."

"What—?" tattoo man spluttered as Ranger closed on them. "Hey, I do my own—"

"Not today. Off with the bra, Shana. We're running out of time."

Tat, if that was his name, continued to protest. Just when she thought the men might come to blows, the woman suggested they work up a scene showing Ranger finding Tat and his captive. "Lot of our old customers, they'll remember Ranger," she explained. "You two can do a territorial thing, you know a competition to see who can get her to come the loudest."

Features sober, Ranger touched Shana's shoulder. "What do you think?"

I want you handling me, bringing me to climax. Only you. I trust you, not him. And yet she'd always wondered what it would be like to have men fighting over her. Also, done right, the video could give her the necessary clout to demand to see Lindsay. She didn't dare lose sight of her goal.

"I don't want sand in my pussy," she said.

The woman hooted. "Sounds like a pro. You tell 'em lady. Don't ever let a man think he's calling the shots."

After a short discussion, everyone decided that using a large beach towel for at least the most intimate part of the shoot wouldn't look too hokey. While Shana handed her bra to the woman and started in on her nylons, Ranger and Tat outlined the next scene. Listening to them, she almost believed they were discussing how to repair a fence. Maybe she could do the same thing. After all, she'd spent countless shoots acting as if she was in love with her outfits. No matter which man handled her, she'd play to the camera, do her act.

Or could she after what Ranger had put her through in the last few days?

When Tat put the previously unused metal around her waist, she felt herself being sucked back into a world of sensation and tested limits. Ranger watched while Tat hobbled her legs and put the wrist restraints back on. When Tat hooked the rigid cuffs to a hook at the back of the waist contraption, he asked if it was too uncomfortable.

"No." In truth, not being able to move her arms the slightest bit was an erotic experience. She wished the others would go away so she and Ranger could play, and yet she didn't. Being the center of attention like this — how long before they forced her over the edge?

When the cameras started rolling again, Tat was pushing his captive from behind, laughing at her awkward steps. "Not sure where we'll start the game," he said. "Privacy's important, not just so we don't have to hold back, but because I don't want anyone trying to horn in on my fun."

On cue, Ranger came into view walking toward them.

"Shit," Tat exclaimed. "Not him! Come on bitch, let's roll."

Grabbing her arm, he tried to turn her away from Ranger, but the chain tangled her, and she fell to her knees. By the time she'd righted herself, Ranger stood over her.

"Well, well, well, what do we have here?" Ranger sounded like the evil mustache-twirling man in the *Perils of Pauline* movies. "Looks like you've bagged yourself a prime piece of meat, old buddy. Bet you weren't going to share, were you?"

"Where'd you come from?" Tat retorted. "You said you had business in the city."

"Guess I lied. I knew you were going to do some prowling today and stuck around to see if you bagged anything. You did good, old buddy. Damn good. She put up a fight?"

"Damn right. Why do you think I made sure she'd stay slowed down? What do you want with her? You've got yourself a harem."

"A man can never have enough horseflesh." Ranger stuck out his hand. "What if we call a truce today, both partake of the goodies?"

Tat shrugged and shook. "What the hell, why not? I'll tell you what, you give me first dibs at your harem tonight, and I'll forget who did the work of corralling this one."

Under any other circumstances, she might have laughed at the corny dialogue. But she wondered if Ranger had joined them because he had concerns about her safety. She hoped his motives were more personal, more intimate, but despite his touches and the nerve-jarring kiss, she wasn't sure.

"I'll tell you what," Tat said. "We'll each take a run at her. See who can unhinge her first."

Ranger pretended to consider the challenge. As he mulled things over, he fingered her breasts. "How do we decide who starts? Flip a coin?"

"I'm not that democratic. I caught her, I go first."

"What-what are you going to do?" Shana managed. "Are you going to rape—?"

"Rape isn't necessary here. Never has and never will be." Tat leaned close, his chest pressing against her breasts. "Don't worry, sweet cheeks. By the time I'm done with you, you'll be running after me like a dog in heat."

Not in this lifetime. After a brief discussion, it was decided to gag her so only her body's reactions could be used to measure her responsiveness. Instead of the dreaded ball gag, Tat ran a wooden bar between her teeth and fastened that behind her head with leather attached to the wood. *So this was what a horse felt with a bit in its mouth.* She hadn't so much as contemplated trying to get away because the ankle restraints made it impossible for her to do more than shuffle. Although she couldn't move her arms, she felt little discomfort. In truth, she could hardly wait for the *experiment* to start.

You put me in this position, Ranger, you.

No. The truth was, the last week wouldn't have happened if she hadn't been who she was—a woman hungry for a sexual journey with the right man.

Tat stepped behind her and yanked her toward him. If he hadn't been there to support her, she would have fallen. Taking advantage of her helplessness, he effortlessly sat her down on the blanket. To keep from toppling backward, she bent her knees. Her open-to-the-world pussy made her feel less than human, but she couldn't hide it from the camera's view. Nervous, she watched Tat dig in his bag.

He pulled out a vibrator, surely not one meant for insertion, but an instrument with a large, rounded head. "No time for subtleties, bitch," he said. "I'm getting out the heavy artillery. Let's see you ignore this."

He held it up for her to see, then turned it on. The head turned in rapid circles and vibrated at the same time, the sound so loud she couldn't imagine that much power coming from batteries. Unable to do anything else, she sat and held her breath as he ran his fingers over her pussy lips.

"Wet. Wet and hot. That's a good sign. Means I don't have to waste time warming you up. You ever been played with like this?"

She shook her head.

"First time for everything. Now for some fun."

Although she tried to straighten her legs to prevent easy access, he simply pushed down on a knee and pressed the vibrator against the front of her vagina. With the first touch, she felt hard movement throughout her sexual organs, the most intense impact centered on her clit. She hadn't wanted to react so quickly. In truth, she'd been determined to let Ranger *win*, but if she couldn't soon get away...

Driven by instinct, she struggled to escape. Unfortunately, she started to fall over on her side.

"Ain't gonna do you no good, bitch," Tat announced as he righted her. "Upright or flat on your back, you have no choice in the outcome."

He went back to anchoring one leg to the ground while he continued to cover her with the wonderfully punishing instrument. Sweat broke out on her throat; she could barely breathe. She struggled to focus on Ranger, but her vision blurred. Her belly tightened, and although she succeeded in briefly relaxing the muscles there, the moment he adjusted the vibrator's position, it clenched again.

Her clit felt as if it was being attacked by bees. There was no pain, but the impact remained intense. She tried to close her legs around the instrument of pleasure and agony, but Tat was in control.

Fight, fight, save yourself for Ranger!

I can't-can't!

She'd never climaxed so quickly. Wave after wave passed through her; she bit into the wood and groaned around it. He kept after her, drawing out her release, forcing it to go on and on until she almost lost consciousness.

Driven half-crazy, she struggled to scream.

"Enough!" she heard Ranger order.

Tat ground the vibrator against her for another second or two as her body jumped, and she sobbed, then granted her release.

"Top that," Tat challenged as he brushed her hair out of her eyes. Then he stood and indicated he was turning her over to Ranger. "Shit. Talk about primed. That was one hot broad."

"You bastard," Ranger muttered.

"All's fair in war and war. What about it, Shana? You need a week or two to regain your strength?"

If it had been anyone except Ranger, she'd have begged to be left alone. But as the explosive waves receded, she realized she wasn't spent after all. Hunger, she was discovering, came in many forms. Her body had been satisfied, but Tat hadn't come close to touching her emotions, her heart.

Ranger began by massaging her shoulders and the back of her neck. She relaxed and became unconcerned with the cameras or who might eventually view the video. With Ranger she felt safe and protected despite the bindings. When he knelt behind her, she leaned against his chest, rested the back of her head on his collarbone, and closed her eyes.

You and me, Ranger. Just the two of us, together, exploring, trusting.

He reached over her and turned his magical fingers loose on her breasts. His position reminded her of the erotic and frustrating session under the tree. Behind the wooden gag she made soft mewling sounds and rocked from side to side.

She vaguely caught the sound of ocean waves and an occasional bird, heard her and Ranger's breathing but no one else's. The settling sun turned the world behind her eyelids red and orange, and she attributed the rainbow of colors to a certain man's mastery of her body. His care and concern for her.

When he shifted position, she waited. Funny how she could feel utterly comfortable with no control over her limbs. His hands roamed lower, claiming her belly and hips, brushing the apex to her sex. He rubbed his knuckles against her mons, and when she bucked against him, he chuckled and covered a breast.

"It's just us," he whispered. "Going places we couldn't before, doing what we've both wanted."

She felt consumed by his hands, one quietly sheltering and cradling a breast while the other teased her clit out of its protective hood. No longer dreading her body's response, she let her muscles loosen and grow slack. He had no need to force her legs apart as Tat had done. Instead, she eagerly offered herself to him and welcomed him in.

He caressed her here, there, everywhere, pleasuring her vagina one part at a time until everything flowed together in her mind. She bent her knees further and spread herself as far as the ankle chain allowed, lifting her hips and turning toward his masterful hand. His straining cock ground into her backside.

Fantasy took over. He no longer supported her but had moved around in front and now straddled her, his naked cock poised at the entrance to her pussy. Flat on her back with her bound arms forcing her breasts toward him, she smiled as best she could behind the gag. Flesh pressed against flesh as he housed himself in her. Even as he began fucking her, he continued to massage her breasts.

The image darkened to be replaced by reality. She couldn't tell and didn't care how many times he'd moved inside her. Only movement mattered. He stroked and prodded, retreated and gifted her again. Something, probably his thumb, repeatedly flicked her clit.

"Give into it, Shana," he chanted. His voice sounded less than steady. "Go with what we both want."

I want you-you joining me in climax.

Perhaps he read her mind because, without taking his fingers out of her, he scrambled around until he was at her side. Without his body holding her, she fell back onto the blanket, and as had happened in her fantasy, her breasts were offered up to him, her willing and hot vagina her gift to him.

He leaned over her and pulled first a nipple and then as much of her breast as he could into his mouth. Simultaneously, his imbedded fingers continued their intimate search. The heel of his hand ground against her mons.

She was going! Letting loose!

Her pussy wept and stained the blanket, drenching his hand at the same time. Her neck arched. She stared up at the sunset, lost herself in the brilliant colors, and howled.

Chapter Fifteen

"So who's the winner?"

Shana pulled the blanket around her nude and sandy body, but although she should care about the answer, she didn't. Satisfied and exhausted, it had barely sunk in that the chains, cuffs, and gag had been removed, and the photographers were putting their equipment away.

"Guess we'll have to let the customers decide," Ranger answered Tat's question.

"Take a poll," the woman photographer suggested. "But in my book, it's a slam dunk. Ranger, if you ever want to try out any new techniques, I'm volunteering to be your guinea pig. How about it, Shana? Float your teeth, did he?"

Her teeth indeed felt loose, prompting her to chuckle and nod agreement. "Awesome," she admitted.

"Because I primed your pump," Tat muttered. "No fair you coming second, Ranger. The way I'd left her, a monkey could have gotten her to climax."

Maybe she should have demanded Tat stop with the crude comments, but until she'd had more time to pull herself together—"What happens now?" she finally thought to ask.

"You mean in regards to your future at Scarlet Cavern?" Tat gave her shoulder a companionable pat. "Talk to management." He nodded in the direction of the deck. "And play hardball. You can name your price."

The male photographer asked Tat to check something on his equipment, and since the woman was already heading back toward the house, she and Ranger were suddenly alone. "What happens now?" she repeated, fighting the urge to ask him to hold her. From the moment she'd come, he'd treated her as if she was nothing more than a subject, a frightening prospect.

"You heard Tat."

"That's not what I'm talking about." For the first time she noted a number of people standing on the deck looking down at them. "When do I get to see Lindsay?"

"Not long." He turned her toward him, gripping her shoulders almost painfully. "You liked it, didn't you? The whole scene."

"What's not to like? Maybe-maybe it's different for men, but lots of women fantasize about forced sex. Speaking from personal experience, it's mind-blowing."

"Something you could get addicted to?"

"No question about it."

"You want to become a Cavern model?"

A model? Was that what it was? "I-I'd better not answer until I've had time to put things in perspective." Even as she spoke, her pussy responded to the prospect of a repeat performance. She wasn't particularly into whips, but well-aimed slaps would indeed get the blood flowing and make a climax even more intense. How was Tat with whips? *Forget Tat!*

"You passed your test, Shana, not that I ever had any doubt." Ranger continued to hold her. "As Tat said, management is going to offer you a contract."

A document legitimizing a primitive act seemed laughable, or maybe it would have if Ranger hadn't been serious. Daylight was nearly gone, the sunset fading. In a few minutes, she wouldn't be able to read his expression. "You-you never said anything about that before."

"Because I didn't want to influence your decision."

But you want to, I can sense it.

"What are you saying?" she asked.

Before he could answer, if he intended to, a familiar male voice called out their names. It took her a moment to place it—Damek.

"Let's do this," Ranger said and all but dragged her toward the deck.

* * * * *

"He prepared you well, didn't he?" Damek asked as he and the two other owners of the Cavern faced Ranger and Shana across the patio table.

"Excuse me?" Shana said.

"Our man Ranger here." Damek chuckled. "Watching you earlier, there's no doubt he knows how to prime a woman's pump. Being brought repeatedly to climax is addictive, isn't it?"

Although he knew how she'd respond, Ranger dreaded hearing the words. He felt as if he was losing touch with her—had already lost touch. With few, very few exceptions, the women who spent time in the Cavern experiencing everything it had to offer became addicted to a state of constant sexual arousal. As proof of how far Shana had already progressed, she'd said nothing about wanting clothes. He could smell sex on her and knew he'd find her pussy still sopping. What did she care about a shower? She was probably already fantasizing about her next—session.

Why are you complaining? You did your job damn well. She might even give you a bonus, or maybe pay you to play with her some more. Explain that to the IRS — job description, stud.

Only, he didn't just want to be a stud with Shana.

"I don't know how you do it," Mark Brewster said. "Your father told me you were the key to our success. He handled the business end of things; you provided the necessary products. You're sure you won't come back?"

If that's the only way I can stay around Shana, maybe. But no matter much he wanted her in his life and bed, he'd already seen all the public display of her sexuality he ever wanted to. If he couldn't have her to himself, if he couldn't keep her satisfied and get to know more about her as a human being, take her to his log home and walk through the woods with her, what had sprung to life between them would die. And when it did, he'd wish her well.

"You know the answer," he shot out. "I'm not interested."

"Pity. So Shana, what's your schedule like? How much time can you give us? Our clients will want to see as much of you as possible. Of course, you'll want to monitor that for awhile. A girl needs her rest, doesn't she? Time to recuperate."

"Let me get this straight," she said in a voice devoid of emotion. "One — audition, I guess you call it — and you believe I have what it takes?"

"Not just one," Damek pointed out. "Don't forget, I got a sneak preview. I let the others know what I saw." He indicated Mark and Samuel Carson who'd been Ranger's father's stockbroker before he'd decided to join the *business*. "We've had a few failures — and one bad experience — but nowadays the screening process is comprehensive. To answer your question, yes, you have what it takes. How's that for an offer—rich and happy at the same time?"

Barely breathing, Ranger waited for Shana's response. He tried to tell himself he was ready to hear the words he was sure he would, but if his clenched fists were any indication, he wasn't. Shana had gone into this because she was worried about her friend. Back then, before he'd come to care for her, he hadn't given a damn what she did. Now that it was too late and she'd discovered the full extent of her sexuality, he wished he hadn't agreed to have anything to do with her.

"It's tempting," she said, her voice still neutral. "But before I agree to anything, I'd like to talk to some other...models."

"Hmm," Mark muttered. "What for?"

Under the table, Shana laid her hand on Ranger's thigh. Muscles tense, he refused to respond.

"There's a fine line here," she said after a short silence, "between pleasure and pain, willingness and coercion. I need to know how other women feel about the experience."

Samuel chuckled. "Spoken like a businesswoman. Get the facts before signing on the bottom line."

But she will, Ranger acknowledged, then struggled to catch up with the conversation.

"And I want to choose who I talk to, not have someone spout the party line."

"She's tough," Damek said, his voice revealing his admiration. "So do you have anyone in mind? I didn't think you'd met any of the other models."

"Not here I haven't," Shana said. Ranger caught the

tension in her voice but doubted anyone else did. "I checked out the website, at least as much as I could. You had several teasers—one showing a slender blonde with strings tied around her nipples."

"Lindsay," Damek said.

"Yes, Lindsay. I want to talk to her, alone."

* * * * *

"That didn't take you long. Good job."

She and Ranger were sitting on the deck now lit by several muted lights. Damek had explained that Lindsay was staying at the place, and he'd see if she was free. Someone had handed her her clothes, and although she hadn't bothered with the silly garter belt and nylons or killer heels, she felt semi-dressed in the see-through blouse and short skirt. Although the others had invited her and Ranger to join them in the dining room, he'd said they'd rather eat out here, and she hadn't complained.

However, until now Ranger hadn't spoken to her. They still sat at the same table, but he'd taken a chair across from her. If she told him she'd far preferred his method of bringing her to climax to Tat's and could hardly wait for the next time, what would he say? His hard cock had left no doubt he'd been aroused, but maybe the reaction had been strictly primal.

And if she admitted she longed for more than sex from him?

"You mean about getting to talk to Lindsay," she finally thought to say.

"Yeah. I didn't know she was staying here. Sounds like she prefers this to anywhere else."

A few days ago she wouldn't have believed Lindsay was here of her own free will. Now she couldn't say. "Like they said, if a model has nothing else going on at the time — "

"Not just that."

His tone silenced her.

"Think about it." He sounded angry. "If you're one hundred percent into sex, what better place to live than in the middle of the action?"

Suddenly ill, she put down her forkful of chicken. "You don't much like her, do you?"

"I don't know her. I'm not going to make assumptions."

"You already have!"

"Maybe. The way you keep defending her, telling yourself she's being held against her will — "

"I don't want to talk about this!"

"Then what?"

Hoping to give herself time to think, she picked up her fork and nibbled. "What happens afterward?" she whispered.

When he said nothing, she retreated inside herself. She'd hired this man to help her contact her best friend, but he'd done much, much more. Not only had he guided her into the world Lindsay occupied, he'd shown her things about her body she'd never imagined — awakened it in ways both exciting and frightening.

The real question, maybe the only one that mattered — how would she face her tomorrows? With him no longer in her life and on and in her body, was there any point?

"Shana?"

At the sound of Lindsay's voice, she sprang to her feet. The quiet light kept her friend's features in shadow, and she wore a loose-fitting shirt and sweats that hid her body. All too aware that Ranger was watching, Shana turned and faced the woman she'd changed her life for.

"How did you find me?" Lindsay asked. Her hands were at her sides, fingers clenched.

"The truth?"

"Yeah."

"All right. I came across the Scarlet Cavern site."

"Come across? What do you mean?"

"I was killing time one evening, trying to add visual stimulation to what I was doing with my vibrator."

"Oh."

A moment ago she'd been nearly speechless; now a thousand questions tumbled through her. Still, this had to be done in private. "Lindsay, this is—"

"I know who he is. I've seen videos of his work."

"He, ah, I hired him to help me get to you."

"And now you have? What do you want from me?"

* * * * *

Ranger had said nothing when Shana asked Lindsay if they could go where they'd have privacy. As Lindsay led the way inside, Shana had looked back at Ranger. Even now, sitting in Lindsay's bedroom, she couldn't shake the image of his strong, silent form.

Lindsay's bedroom, a suite really, was decorated in burgundy and white. The matching recliners they now sat in were nearly new and obviously expensive. The queen-sized bed came with a feminine canopy, but what kept running through Shana's mind was what use Lindsay and the men she allowed in here might put the four posters to.

Several floral-scented candles burned on a windowsill. The other window had a small greenhouse built into it and was alive with miniature roses. Three oil paintings of ocean scenes served as the only wall decoration. Each spoke of wild weather and storm-tossed waves, the colors an exquisite mix of silver, blues, and white.

"They're beautiful," she said of the paintings.

"Thank you. I'm working on another with a sail ship in it."

"You painted these? Lindsay, I had no idea you—"

"Neither did I until I stopped running from myself, telling myself I had it together when I didn't—until I became free." Lindsay tucked her legs under her, revealing red toenails.

"Free?"

"Not the way you're thinking. Kid, I know what film clips of me are on the site. They give the impression I'm—how shall we say it?—being held against my will. That's what brought you here, isn't it? You wanted to rescue me."

"I was so scared for you. I imagined...all kinds of things."

"Yes, I'm sure you did. Let me ask you something, all right."

She nodded.

"How long have you been with Ranger?"

"Ah, less than a week, why?"

"What's the nature of your relationship?"

Lindsay had never minced words. Besides, Shana didn't want to beat around the bush either. "I hired him, among other things, to demonstrate what Scarlet Cavern is like."

"He's the master."

"Yes, he is." Flames heated her cheeks, but she didn't try to hide her reaction.

"He'd left long before I came here," Lindsay said. "But everything the others do is modeled after his work. I used to—hell—I still fantasize about him working me." She leaned forward. "Are you disgusted? You think I've sold my soul to the devil? Maybe you believe I'm worse than a whore."

"I don't know what to think," she said although maybe she did.

Lindsay placed her hands between her knees and began rocking. "You know what my childhood was like — and that I've always bounced around—looking for some place to belong."

"You've built a career for yourself. The ponds you design—"

"I'm proud of them, but, well, having to bid on jobs, the competition, problems with supplies, trying to satisfy clients, asking myself how long I can physically do the work—"

"Why didn't you tell me how you felt?"

"Because you bankrolled me." She dripped her gaze. "How many times have I come running to you for support? I couldn't bring myself to admit I still hadn't found myself."

"Found?"

"I was still drifting, making more money than I ever had before, but drifting, restless."

Galvanized by the pain in Lindsay's voice, Shana

stood, then dropped to her knees in front of her. "Why did you think you couldn't share that with me? I would have understood, supported—"

"Supported? Believe me, there were times—like when I was a nickel from living on the street—that I wanted nothing more than to put myself in your hands, to let you become my parent. But that isn't healthy. Shana, I needed to find out who I am."

I think, maybe, I've just finished the same journey. I just didn't know I was on one.

"Why didn't you say anything about Scarlet Cavern?"

"How? Drop by one day and tell you I was showing my cunt to the world?"

She took Lindsay's hands and began rubbing them; they felt so cold. "Don't put it that way."

"It's the way people talk in this industry. I can't pretend to be anything except what I am. I just—hell, you know me in ways no one else ever will. I didn't tell you what I was up to because I didn't know how to answer your questions. I thought—hell, for all I knew you'd haul me off to some shrink or reject me for what I was doing; I couldn't handle that. As for explaining why I love having orgasms forced on me—I'm not sure I understand myself. It is a kick; I'll give you that."

Although she wanted to continue warming Lindsay's hands, Shana stood and walked over to the rose-filled window. "You never cared about flowers before."

"It's not that. I just never saw them as part of my life. So much has changed in the last year."

"Tell me about it, please. How did it start?"

Lindsay frowned then briefly closed her eyes as if looking deep inside herself. "I'm trying to—you were off modeling somewhere. One of my clients invited me to join her and some friends to a wet T-shirt contest. I thought, why the hell not. I drank, not much but enough so I didn't think twice when I joined the fun. There was some bump and grind music, and I started moving to it, pretending like I was a pole dancer or something. I won the contest. Then as we were leaving, the manager gave me his card and told me to call him if I wanted to have fun and make some money."

"He was associated with Scarlet Cavern?"

"Kind of. He's a rigger for them, does a lot of the rope work. He started by giving me videos of some of the shoots and told me to watch them when I was alone. They were incredible. I imagined myself being *done*. Shana, I've never felt more-more alive I guess. When I finally calmed down, I called him and asked what I needed to do."

"And the more involved you became, the more hesitant you were to tell me?"

"Yes. I didn't want you thinking I'd become perverted."

"You didn't think I'd understand, did you?"

"You'd ask questions. You'd deserve answers and I wasn't sure I could provide them."

"I'm here now. And I understand — a lot."

"Do you? What you did in order to reach me — it doesn't disgust you? That's why...you have no idea how hard it was not to let you know I was here. I am so damned ashamed of having put you through this."

She could have told Lindsay that her reactions had been a world away from disgust, but she wanted the focus on her friend. "I hope I've never criticized you, and you've always supported my decisions. I just want you to be at peace with yourself."

"At peace?" Lindsay blinked rapidly. "I've changed. Not just because I now shave my pussy every day, but because I feel closer to myself, in touch."

"You're happy?" Shana asked.

"Happy? It's more than I've ever had. I've stopped running from shadows and letting the past control me. The rapes happened years ago. It's damn time I got over them."

"I've always wanted that for you."

"I know you have. You just didn't go at it the right way."

"Because I didn't take you to a wet T-shirt contest?"

"Or tie me up and plant a vibrator on me." She laughed. "I'm indulging myself, growing. And I'm getting some killer climaxes."

"They are mind-blowing, aren't they?" Shana admitted. Had she ever felt so close to her friend, so open?

Lindsay stood and joined her at the window. "I watched you today. Became a damn voyeur complete with binoculars."

"You did?" She couldn't make herself meet Lindsay's gaze.

"I didn't want you to lose your concentration, but you want the truth? I nearly came thinking about joining in on the action."

Maybe she should be shocked. Instead, her crotch began to ache. She'd gone into this because she needed to understand Lindsay's new world. She hadn't expected her own to change, to come to life in ways she hadn't known possible. "Can I ask you something?"

Lindsay nodded.

"Everything you do, it's entirely of your own free will? The chains and ropes and whips—"

"Don't forget gags and nipple and pussy clamps. Yes, I approve of everything that's done. Hell, more and more I get to decide what's going to happen in the shoot. I have one coming up next week in which—are you ready for this?"

For what? "Yes," she said, driven by the heat between her legs.

"All right." Showing no sign of self-consciousness, Lindsay pulled her shirt over her head, cupped her hands under her naked breasts, and lifted them. Her nipples had been pierced, delicate silver rings protruding from them.

"My—did it hurt?"

"Like hell. What a high! What do you think?"

Not giving herself time to question her action, Shana fingered the rings. "Can you remove them?"

"No." Lindsay's voice turned husky. "Unless I or someone else takes cutters to them, my boobs will stay imprisoned. It's…I've enslaved myself. Only it doesn't feel that way. I'm free to be a sexual creature. Right now that's enough."

She should release her friend's breasts and go back to asking questions, pretend she wasn't becoming more and more excited. She couldn't.

"Like the feeling?" Lindsay purred. "Knowing you can easily control me?"

"Y-es."

"I love it too. Knowing that if a man—or woman—takes hold of the rings, I have to do whatever they want.

Maybe it's sick, but I don't care. For the first time in my life, I like my body. Hell, I love what it does for me."

She could hook chains to the rings and lead Lindsay around, turn her into her own private slave. Maybe she'd fasten Lindsay to one of the bed posters by her breasts, tie her hands and legs—spread wide of course—and force a climax out of her best friend.

"It'd—you'd be so vulnerable."

"I've been vulnerable all my life. And a victim for too much of it. But now—even if you think it's sick—this is my decision, not something someone else forced on me."

Part of her knew Lindsay was still a small, lost child. But instead of destroying her life with drugs or booze, Lindsay had tapped into something deep inside her and turned weakness into strength—at least the kind of strength that would sustain her.

"I want you happy," she whispered and forced her hands back to her sides.

"I want the same for you," Lindsay said and hugged her.

"We're still friends, soul sisters?" she asked.

Lindsay nodded. "That's the only thing I haven't liked about what I'm doing—believing I'd driven a wedge between us."

"It doesn't have to be like that. I won't let it."

"You mean it?" Lindsay sounded on the verge of tears.

"With all my heart." She returned the embrace. "We've gone through too much to let anything get in the way of our friendship. I understand-understand what you've embraced. If it fulfills you, I'll support it."

"Thank you," Lindsay muttered. "You have no idea how much I've needed to hear that. If—do you think you'd like to watch my next shoot?"

"I'll be there."

* * * * *

Ranger was still on the deck when Shana returned. The door had opened soundlessly, making her wonder if he knew she was there. Perhaps not because he hadn't moved from his position by the railing. He was studying the ocean now softly lit by a half moon. Was he contemplating how soon he could leave here—and her?

"She's all right," Shana said. She couldn't make herself leave the safety of the doorway. "Much better than I ever thought she'd be."

"You couldn't convince her to leave?" he asked without turning around.

"I didn't try. Thanks to you, I understand how addictive this lifestyle can become."

"Addictive and seductive."

Seductive. The word flowed through her, sent strength to her legs, and propelled her forward. Careful not to risk touching him, she joined him in studying the watery world in the distance. "It's beautiful. Lindsay says that's why she stays here, so she can walk on the beach and listen to the wind and waves."

"It's not the only reason."

"I know." If only she could tap into his emotions—and understand her own. "Like you say, the lifestyle is seductive." Before she knew she was going to do it, she touched his arm. He turned toward her but kept his hands on the railing. "I've changed because of you," she admitted. "You taught me things about my body I never suspected — things — needs I can't turn my back on."

"I didn't think you could."

His comment puzzled her, but she suspected he wouldn't supply one if she asked for an explanation.

"They want you bad," Ranger said.

"What?"

"Damek and Mark talked to me while you were with Lindsay. They asked how much they'd have to offer to get you to sign a two-year contract."

"Two years?"

"They've never done that before, committed themselves to a long-term arrangement with a woman." He turned his attention back to the ocean. "The camera loves you. You hold nothing back. You have a beautiful, responsive body."

Maybe she should feel flattered, but all she could think of was whether she'd see Ranger after tonight.

"What did you tell them?"

"That I don't speak for you."

Because you don't want to? "What are *you* going to do? They want you back too."

"They aren't getting me."

Although the thought of surrendering her body and sexuality to Ranger while cameras recorded the magic he produced in her made her hot, she didn't try to change his mind.

"I-I'm grateful for everything you did for me," she said putting off the moment when they'd part. "You had to bring me to the edge of sanity for me to understand- understand why Lindsay is doing what she is."

"I did what you hired me for."

"And now you're angry. Why?"

He whirled on her, capturing her wrists before she could react. He turned her from him, pulling her arms behind her at the same time. His large hand easily held her wrists, and he forced her to lean forward. She felt his lips on the back of her neck, the contact feather-light and fleeting. Still, she felt it all the way to her soul. Then he groaned, and his body tensed. After hiking her short skirt over her buttocks, he slid a hand between her legs. For a moment she tried to clamp her legs together. Then heat and trust took over, and she surrendered. *Do whatever you want*, she silently told him. *All I ask is some tenderness, another kiss. Talk about our future.*

"It takes so little to turn you on," he said and removed his hand. "I'll take credit for some of it but not all. You're hardwired to respond, highly sexed."

"What's your point?"

"My point?" He pulled her upright, yanked down her skirt and released her. "You're crazy if you don't take them up on their offer. Getting your kicks whenever you want, having Tat work on you—he can hardly wait to have another run at you."

"A run at me?" She threw the disgusting term back at Ranger.

"Call it what you want." He gripped the railing with white knuckles the faint light couldn't hide. "The stupid contest he and I had earlier? I don't know what the hell I was thinking, maybe that only I could get you off anymore. But he—and you—proved me wrong. You screamed for Tat. Damn near blew the top of your head off."

"Is this what that's about?" she demanded. "You're angry because Tat got me to climax."

Ignoring her, he leaned against the railing.

"Why do you care?" she whispered. "I'm just a client to you, after all. It's what you keep telling me."

"Yeah." His whisper was no stronger than hers. "A client."

"What about when we had sex? That wasn't supposed to be part of the arrangement. Our talks—you telling me about your relationship with your father—more outside the scope of our contract, right?"

"Yeah."

"Why?" She stared at his dark profile. "Why did things cross over the line between us?"

He straightened. As he turned toward her, his shoes whispered on the decking. "I don't know." He sighed. "No, I'm not going to lie. You were willing to risk a great deal for someone you love. I've never seen that kind of sacrifice before. And the way you entrusted your body to me, not for money and sexual satisfaction the way the women here do, but because you needed to understand what Lindsay had embraced—"

"At the beginning I didn't know it was a matter of *embracing*."

"I loved being your teacher," he admitted. "But before long things changed. I trusted you the same way you did me. I told you about the place I built. I even—I even thought about taking you there."

He trusted her? Exposed his vulnerability to her? Overwhelmed by love, she stood on tiptoe and locked her arms around his neck. Her breasts, constrained by the push-up-and-out bra, strained for him. When he wrapped his arms around her and held her close—letting her feel his erection—everything she'd ever embraced about self-preservation melted away. When he returned her kiss, she whimpered low in her throat.

Behind her, the ocean ran endlessly up and down the shoreline, but she only dimly sensed the tide. Everything else remained locked on Ranger, loving him, sharing with him.

"I had two climaxes—so far—today," she told him. "One Tat forced from me because he has tools and knows a woman's triggers. The other—you knew what I needed, the right touches, being embraced, feeling safe."

"I wanted to give you…"

"You did." She ran her hands under his shirt, heating her fingertips on his chest. "You gave me a gift. And now it's my turn."

"Your turn?"

Giddy, she led him toward the stairs. "To pleasure you. For starters. Ranger, I'd love to see your place. For a long time now I've thought about buying a real home instead of living in a condo, no longer living out of suitcases. You turned your life in another direction. Can you understand why I want to do the same thing?"

He held back. "If we have sex tonight, I'll want you in my life from now on. But I can't share you with the world. I won't. If you sign that contract, you'll become a wealthy woman. You can buy any place you want."

"I already have more money than I need," she told him. "But money isn't enough. I need—I want what you've shown me."

"This?" He indicated the massive house.

"No! It was exciting, I can't deny that. But if you'll

have me, you're the only audience I'll ever scream for again."

Epilogue

"Leave it to Lindsay," Shana said as she held up the discreetly wrapped package. "Whatever she's sent us, something tells me it's best opened in private."

"It might be for you," Ranger said from the living room where he was securing a loose leg on the couch they'd just bought. "You know, one woman's joke gift to another."

"No, it's addressed to both of us. How are things going?"

"Fine." Ranger turned the couch upright. "It just wasn't screwed in tight. Well, what do you think of our first purchase as an old engaged couple?"

Engaged. Despite the simple diamond on her left hand, she could barely believe she and Ranger would be getting married in less than a month. Their relationship had been a whirlwind of emotions and experiences. They'd be honeymooning in Alaska followed shortly after by a move to Florida. She'd miss a lot about San Diego and had fallen in love with Ranger's log cabin, but with Recovery establishing an office near Miami and in need of a manager, the timing was right for him to put distance between himself and his past. She could design girls' athletic clothing anywhere.

Holding the package, she joined Ranger. She hadn't been sure about a leather couch, but when she'd seen him looking both masculine and relaxed on in it, she'd happily given her approval. Besides, as he'd pointed out, it was large enough for two—both vertical and horizontal.

"So, old lady, what's the gift?"

"Old lady!" she snorted and shoved him onto the couch. As she'd suspected—hoped—he pulled her down on his lap. "If I'm an old lady, you know what that makes you."

"Yeah." He nibbled the side of her neck. "Your stud."

"In your dreams."

"And everywhere else we can think of," he pointed out.

Knowing he was right, she pretended great interest in the gift. Inside the silver and black wrapping was a small, carved wooden box. She lifted the lid.

"She would!" she exclaimed. "Only Lindsay."

"What is it?" Ranger asked as he removed the gold chain and attached clamps.

"What do you mean, what is it?" she snorted. "You know darn well."

"I'm not sure. Let me think about it." He held the intimate piece of jewelry up to her breasts. "No. Doesn't fit there. The design of the clamps is wrong. Maybe another part of your anatomy..." He finished by sliding a hand between her legs. "Yes, I do believe it'll work there."

Although she was looking forward to calling Lindsay and pretending to be scandalized, Shana stood and slipped out of her slacks and underpants. She spread her legs in invitation. "What do you think?" she asked. "Any chance they'd stay on my nether lips?"

"Even wet, my dear, even wet. You want a demonstration?"

She did — and they did.

Enjoy this excerpt from
Thunder

© Copyright Vonna Harper 2002

All Rights Reserved, Ellora's Cave Publishing, Inc.

Chapter 1

The storm flung itself at Mala Bey's car. Attacking, sometimes shrieking, it buffeted her small vehicle until Mala was forced to slow to thirty miles an hour. Her windshield wipers were all but useless.

Blue-black, the cloud-choked sky dominated everything. Occasionally, Mala glimpsed a sliver of gold on the horizon which gave her hope that the entire world wasn't locked in this furious Florida afternoon storm, but she had little time to reflect on anything except making sure she didn't skid off the highway and plunge into the Everglades lurking on either side.

Alligator Alley. If she got out of this alive, she'd get in touch with whoever was responsible for naming highways and tell them they hadn't gotten it right. This too-thin thread of civilization cutting east to west through southern Florida should go by something like *Hell's Back Yard. Dark Deception. Thunder —*

Crack!!

The explosion worked in harmony with the fingers of brilliant light erupting on the sky. As a native of a state regularly attacked by violent weather, she should be used to the power and overwhelming energy. But, except for a handful of vehicles plowing through the deluge, she was alone in a savage and primal land. The storm wouldn't last long, and the sun would return to bake and steam the earth. She should have waited to travel from Naples to

Fort Lauderdale, but a huge chunk of her future lay at the end of this highway.

The sky became both beautiful and powerful as lightning slashed and scarred. It seemed to hold, then grow and shudder, sending out endless fingers of fire. Although she'd told herself to be ready for the next cannon shot, when it came, she barely stifled a squeak. The car shuddered; she would swear it briefly lost contact with the road. She wanted to pull over and wait out the anger and energy, but if she did, she'd have to park near the encroaching Everglades. For reasons she didn't want to examine, that frightened her more than driving through lightning and thunder and punishing downpour.

Frightened...or something else?

Creatures that should have never been spawned dwelled in the Everglades. Alligators, panthers, snakes — massive, slithering, silent snakes. That's what upset her, not the sense that she was about to be challenged or changed.

Once again lightning rent the sky. The incredible display called her to it.

Now going little more than twenty miles an hour, she headed arrow-like toward the blue and black horizon. A moment ago she'd been terrified; terror now turned into fascination. This monster of energy and might held her in its grip. She gave herself up to it as she'd long dreamed of giving herself, totally and without will or thought, to a man and became nothing except nerves and sight and hearing.

In that secret dream she walked naked and hot with need toward a dark, faceless man. His powerful body hummed, challenged, promised. Urged by his silent command, she'd dropped to her knees before his spread legs and lowered her head in submission. Waiting for him to claim her.

When he gripped her hair and forced her to look up at him, her body heated even more. Became less hers. She immediately arched her back and offered him her breasts, which he took in his large, rough hands. The work-hardened paws claimed her breasts, flattening her swollen nipples against his palms. He began a demanding, slow circular motion that brought her to a place somewhere between pain and climax. Her clit swelled and became wet, and with breath and eyes, she begged him to thrust his cock into her. To end the wanting. He wore only tight black briefs, and his hard penis filled it. But she knew not to touch him until he gave her permission.

But then…

Movement on her left pulled Mala back from the brink of madness and ecstasy, burying but not killing the fantasy and her unchecked reaction. She was being passed, not by a car, but a death-black motorcycle. Its rider crouched low over the beast like an Indian riding a wild stallion—or a man riding a woman. Maybe her. He wore a helmet so dark it was nearly impossible to determine where it left off and the thunder-born landscape began. If it hadn't been for the clear facemask, she might not know whether a man or woman was on board.

A man.

He passed slowly, not cautiously so much as if he was determined to get an intimate look at her and didn't care how long it took, or whether exceeding her speed put him in jeopardy. She tried to take her eyes off him, but the man held her with something, maybe nothing more than an extension of the forces which existed around and above and beyond them.

She took in his bulk, the power and size and agility of him and wondered if any woman had ever tamed the wildness she sensed in him. If she might be that woman. The motorcycle, lean and sleek and dangerous, seemed hard-put to battle wind and rain. A lesser man would have been forced to stop, or been blown off the road before he could.

Not this panther-man.

Her gaze didn't waver from him until he'd passed; nothing else mattered during those seconds when their eyes met and locked and communicated something which now rode deep and hot in her belly.

It couldn't be; she wasn't feeling sexual excitement! *Yeah, right.*

He was a stranger, a damn fool risking his life on an all but deserted highway in danger of being overtaken by the ravenous jungle. He couldn't possibly sense that he embodied her secret and unattainable fantasy.

He was arrogant and self-confident, a physical creature who leaped from one adventure to another, one sexual partner after another, seeking release for his boundless energy. Whether there really were such men, or whether they simply existed deep and untapped and usually unacknowledged in her subconscious, she didn't know, didn't care.

He was man. Animal. Sex. Storm and darkness, woven seamlessly into the environment.

Now he was ahead of her. He'd eased up a little as if he'd sensed her speed and easily matched his to hers the way her dream master-lover knew how to bring her to the brink of climax again and again—to extend the awful, sweet torture. She could tell he was a large man, well over six feet with shoulders so wide that if she tried to wrap her arms around them, she'd be hard pressed to do so. A man like that could never be controlled. He was a master of control.

Get a grip, right now!

He wore nothing to protect himself from the liquid spear points slamming into him. The lack of a coat didn't surprise her. Even in the midst of a storm, the temperature seldom dropped below eighty degrees. Still, his bare hands and arms and throat must be taking a terrible beating. It occurred to her that her vehicle would provide him with protection and wondered why he'd passed instead of remaining behind her.

He looked over his shoulder. Again those eyes, all but hidden under their Plexiglas protection, reached for her, grabbed hold of the hungry woman in her and said something silent, and elemental, and undeniable.

She took in several open-mouthed breaths and tried to force her attention on what had brought her out here today, but the case filled with silver and abalone jewelry which rode on the seat beside her no longer mattered except this rain slickened highway, the dark unknown on either side. The panther-man ahead of her.

Mostly the man.

She was now going just under twenty miles an hour, her speed determined by the motorcyclist. He must have realized he'd made a mistake by passing and wanted back the scant rain-break her car provided. After several minutes of indecision, she pulled into the passing lane.

Keeping far to the left to reduce the amount of water her tires threw at him, she touched the gas pedal.

He was looking at her again, those shadowed eyes sealing them together. Something that tasted too much like fear invaded her. She absorbed it until it changed into need that found a home at the joining of her legs. The heat she now felt had nothing to do with outside temperatures and everything to do with desire and fantasy.

Fantasy.

The rain would cease. He'd stop his motorcycle. She'd pull over next to him and get out. He'd dismount, take off his helmet, revealing ebony hair and eyes which carried the same compelling color, and spear her with his gaze. He'd reach out his hand, not in question but command. She'd place hers in it, warm and strong and wet, leather against silk. With him leading the way, they'd step into the jungle. The jungle would absorb them.

"Strip," he'd say. "Now."

And she would. The civilized woman whose days were filled with trying to earn a living would cease to exist. Instead, she'd allow herself the heady freedom of focusing totally on her body, and on his. To hell with responsibility! Her heart would beat like a drum in a hard-rock band. She'd stare at his totally naked body, not a quick and furtive glance but bold and open because he belonged to her...just as she belonged to him. It would be night, endless night and endless sex.

That's enough! Get a grip!

She was ahead of him. Feeling less in control than she imagined possible, she concentrated on the complex task of herding her car back to the right. After a moment, she again saw him in her rear view mirror. The storm showed no sign of exhausting itself, and she told herself that the least she could do was run interference for this reckless rider. He'd be grateful for her thoughtfulness. He'd —

This wasn't a man ruled by gratitude. Not gentle. Confident of his power over women.

How she'd come to that conclusion didn't matter. This was her fantasy. Hadn't her creativity always been ignited by the colors and sounds and messages of nature?

Only today, a man who was both stallion and panther, not nature, held her. She tried to imagine him in suit and tie responding to voice mail and faxes, hunched over a computer, corporate decisions an everyday occurrence.

No. This was a physical man; what she'd seen of his shoulders, back, arms, and legs told her that. He earned his living with the strength in that work-honed body.

The possibility that he shared his world with a woman nearly made her scream. Hands locked around the steering wheel, she entertained the image of ripping out that woman's throat. Reminding herself that he wasn't hers to claim, she tried to imagine where he lived, whether he walked into an empty house at the end of the day or…Why should she feel this way about a man she didn't know?

Not a house. A boat.

Where that thought came from she couldn't say, but it fit with what her imagination was creating. He'd fall asleep lulled by waves and the sound of seabirds. He knew and loved and accepted the rhythm of the ocean. Maybe he was the descendent of pirates.

A pirate took what he wanted. Armed with knives and confidence, he'd seize a woman and throw her, bound and helpless, onto his boat. He'd stand over her, legs widespread to reveal the awesome size of his penis. Fear would weaken his captive's limbs and when he knelt and straddled her, she'd beg for mercy.

Mercy? He didn't know the meaning of the word.

Mala was telling herself she'd taken the fantasy over the edge when she realized she couldn't see him. She panicked, terrified he'd hit something or been knocked off balance by a powerful gust of wind and was being slammed to the pavement.

When he emerged from her blind spot and began to pull alongside again, relief washed through her. That and an appetite for what he was which clawed and demanded. She looked over at him, nodding casually in the hope he wouldn't suspect what was taking place inside her. He didn't return her lying nod, and it seemed as if his gaze was a little less remote and disturbing. More knowing.

The rain served as a filmy curtain between them. When lightning burst, she was momentarily blinded. Blinking, she now perceived him as an outline, still strong and competent, too dark. He and the motorcycle had become one; the pavement beneath and wilderness behind and beyond all blended into a nearly indefinable whole.

Crack! Crack!

The twin thunderclaps reminded her of how wrong she was to think she could exert any control over the weather. She waited, a concentration that separated her from the reality of the man she shared the road with. When she looked for him again he was—

Sliding. Motorcycle out of control! Too thin tires fighting to grip slickened pavement. Plowing into the Everglades.

"No!"

About the author:

Vonna welcomes mail from readers. You can write to her c/o Ellora's Cave Publishing at 1337 Commerce Drive, Suite 13, Stow OH 44224.

Why an electronic book?

We live in the Information Age—an exciting time in the history of human civilization in which technology rules supreme and continues to progress in leaps and bounds every minute of every hour of every day. For a multitude of reasons, more and more avid literary fans are opting to purchase e-books instead of paperbacks. The question to those not yet initiated to the world of electronic reading is simply: *why?*

1. *Price.* An electronic title at Ellora's Cave Publishing runs anywhere from 40-75% less than the cover price of the <u>exact same title</u> in paperback format. Why? Cold mathematics. It is less expensive to publish an e-book than it is to publish a paperback, so the savings are passed along to the consumer.

2. *Space.* Running out of room to house your paperback books? That is one worry you will never have with electronic novels. For a low one-time cost, you can purchase a handheld computer designed specifically for e-reading purposes. Many e-readers are larger than the average handheld, giving you plenty of screen room. Better yet, hundreds of titles can be stored within your new library—a single microchip. (Please note that Ellora's Cave does not endorse any specific brands. You can check our website at www.ellorascave.com for customer recommendations we make available to new consumers.)

3. *Mobility.* Because your new library now consists of only a microchip, your entire cache of books can be taken with you wherever you go.

4. *Personal preferences are accounted for.* Are the words you are currently reading too small? Too large? Too...**ANNOYING**? Paperback books cannot be modified according to personal preferences, but e-books can.

5. *Innovation.* The way you read a book is not the only advancement the Information Age has gifted the literary community with. There is also the factor of what you can read. Ellora's Cave Publishing will be introducing a new line of interactive titles that are available in e-book format only.

6. *Instant gratification.* Is it the middle of the night and all the bookstores are closed? Are you tired of waiting days — sometimes weeks — for online and offline bookstores to ship the novels you bought? Ellora's Cave Publishing sells instantaneous downloads 24 hours a day, 7 days a week, 365 days a year. Our e-book delivery system is 100% automated, meaning your order is filled as soon as you pay for it.

Those are a few of the top reasons why electronic novels are displacing paperbacks for many an avid reader. As always, Ellora's Cave Publishing welcomes your questions and comments. We invite you to email us at service@ellorascave.com or write to us directly at: 1337 Commerce Drive, Suite 13, Stow OH 44224.

Discover for yourself why readers can't get enough of the multiple award-winning publisher Ellora's Cave. Whether you prefer e-books or paperbacks, be sure to visit EC on the web at www.ellorascave.com for an erotic reading experience that will leave you breathless.

WWW.ELLORASCAVE.COM

Printed in the United States
30145LVS00001B/28-30